MAHARAJA IN DENIMS

Maharaja in Denims

Khushwant Singh

AMARYLLIS

AMARYLLIS

Copyright © Khushwant Singh 2014

This edition first published in 2014
Third impression 2015

AMARYLLIS

An imprint of Manjul Publishing House Pvt. Ltd.
7/32 Ground Floor, Ansari Road, Daryaganj, New Delhi 110 002
Email: amaryllis@amaryllis.co.in   Website: www.amaryllis.co.in

Registered Office:
10, Nishat Colony, Bhopal 462 003, M.P. - India

Distribution Centres:
Ahmedabad, Bengaluru, Bhopal, Kolkata, Chennai,
Hyderabad, Mumbai, New Delhi, Pune

ISBN: 978-93-81506-43-1

Printed and Bound in India by
Thomson Press (India) Ltd.

For all those innocent lives which were lost
in the name of religion

One

The moment he entered her, Gaitri's moans had sounded more like Lily's. What's more, her cry, 'faster, faster,' had resonated in his head like that of the beautiful dancing girl from Kashmir, Subhu's, 'Maharaj, karo ji (do me).' This completely confused young Hari while he was making love to Gaitri in his plush Sector 5 house in Chandigarh.

'I'm coming, Lily,' his ecstatic cry turned into a painful scream as Gaitri fiercely bit into the nape of his neck, signalling the end of a relationship that had barely lasted four months.

'Fuck off, you son of a bitch!' she shouted immediately after climaxing. Disentangling herself as fast as possible, she ran into the bathroom with her shirt and Levi's jeans clutched to her well-rounded breasts, shrieking, 'Whoever this Lily is, you're welcome to screw her. Have her as much as you want!' she yelled again, devastated by the sudden revelation.

'Listen, don't be crazy,' called out Hari, scratching his head, a bit dazed with the abrupt turn of events.

'Who the heck is Lily?' he thought to himself.

Gaitri, who had already slipped into her clothes, stormed out of the room, and ran towards the porch where her car was parked.

Chander Bhan, the gardener, who had seen her visit Hari Kaka frequently, had never seen Gaitri maidam zip off in her car with such urgency. 'Ram! Ram!' he uttered as he saw the front fender nudge past his favourite palm-tree pot.

'Never seen a girl run out like this from the many that have come and gone,' he thought to himself. Convinced that Kakaji ne kuch gadbar ki hogi (Hari must have done something wrong), he muttered 'Ram Ram' again, this time in an attempt to waive any wrath god might rain on Kakaji after whatever it was he had done.

'What the shit! You mean this big blue-black mark on your neck is no love bite?' asked Rahul, amused by Hari's early morning confession.

'It is, yet it is not,' replied Hari, visualising the events of the previous evening, still so vivid in his head, as the duo walked into the twelve-thirty English class.

'Leave aside screw, I've never even *dated* a girl named Lily. And if that wasn't weird enough, one Subhu also cropped up. She was wearing a dark green jumper over a satin gown kind of a thing which she lifted up when I was doing her,' said Hari, his grin finally returning after nineteen hours. 'I've never seen anyone wearing that kind of ornate jewellery even at the most lavish Indian weddings!'

'Now don't repeat this to anybody; the whole college is busy guessing which girl you laid last night.'

Hari knew exactly what Rahul meant. Since the morning, his love bite had been working as a trophy for him; his college mates urging him to narrate the events... his mastram or horny talk, as they called it. After all, he had achieved a major milestone in his life – having sex as a teenager. Sex is something most teenagers merely fantasise about. It had taken Hari four relationships and two years of hard work to get his first taste of sex.

Well, big deal if Gaitri had left in a huff! She could be won back; better still, her haste in leaving him without giving him a chance to explain his position now left him free to woo Suzanne, the hot chick he had met the other day on the Shatabadi Express while returning from Delhi.

One week later...

'Called the Lion of the Punjab, or Sher-e-Punjab, Ranjit Singh was in every way as remarkable a man as his two contemporaries, Napoleon and Mehmet Ali,' said Professor Deshbeer, as he paced up and down the classroom, seeking reactions from his students.

Close to retiring now, this professor of history had, throughout his career, been very popular amongst his students because of his feisty style of teaching. He was also one of those rare teachers who would wink at you as if to say 'just go for it', if you ever bumped into him while out on a date. Very few students bunked Deshbeer's class.

'Ranjit Singh, who rose from the status of a petty chieftain to become the most powerful Indian ruler was also the first and only Sikh ruler of Punjab,' Deshbeer's voice pitched high and low as he crafted his story. 'His empire extended from Tibet to the deserts of Sindh, and from the Khyber Pass to the Sutlej in the east, with an estimated area of 1,00,436 square miles and a population of five-and-a-half million.

'Now, our ruler of the time also fancied beautiful women,' he said, adding a bit of spice to the lecture in an attempt to gain one hundred percent attention of his class.

'Subhu and Lily,' yelled Hari from one of the back benches, his hand raised as high as possible to take credit.

'Our man on the second-last bench in the third row seems to be well informed about the shauks of the maharaja of Punjab,' said the professor with a smirk, responding to Hari's abrupt intervention.

'So what do you know about Subhu and Lily, young man?' he asked, keen to make the session interactive, a style that had held him in good stead amongst the student community.

'What do you want to know? That I just lost my girlfriend because of these two bitches?' muttered Hari to himself, his mind trying to search for an answer. 'Who... who... who... some hints... how come?' he mumbled, his mind in flashback mode, wavering between the previous week's events and the present imbroglio. 'What was the connection between his bedroom and classroom? Who were they? I don't know them,' Hari reflected finally, embarrassed by the situation.

And what if the professor had seen that love bite on his

neck that had refused to fade away even after a week? He cursed himself for drawing the class's attention to himself and inviting laughter.

'Shit...' he mumbled again.

Professor Deshbeer, catching the profanity as he read the boy's lips and noticing the love bite, did not press him further, and continued.

'Captain W.G. Osborne, military secretary to the governor general of India, has a very fascinating account of Ranjit Singh.

'Osborne, who accompanied other high-ranking British officials on a mission to Ranjit Singh's state in 1838 – with the aim of persuading him to form an alliance with the British – has, in a diary, highlighted those facets of Ranjit Singh that have been largely ignored by his biographers, especially Sikh writers.

'For example, now, since our friend here has cleverly diverted the discussion to the maharaja's harem, contrary to the tribute to the maharaja's achievements that I had planned, Osborne in his notes – observing Ranjit Singh's court – writes that one of these girls, called Lotus, was a rather celebrated character at the court of Lahore.'

'Lily, you mean?' interrupted Hari yet again, as abruptly as he had done before.

'Yes,' replied Deshbeer. 'Ranjit Singh had received her as a tribute from Kashmir in 1836 when she was at the peak of her beauty.' In all probability, the thirty-odd students hoped that the professor would go ahead and slowly strip Lily naked with his words, giving many of them enough detail for self-gratification. Then they would have no need to go to the Sector-17 Inter State Bus Stand to buy pornographic books written by anonymous writers.

'The military secretary, describing a court event, remarks that the raja fell violently in love with her, and he fancied that his affection was as violently returned.'

'Sir, are you referring to General Ventura's sexual overtures towards Lily?' asked Hari, interrupting the professor once again.

'The overture was prompted by the maharaja himself, my dear boy. You stand corrected, as it was the maharaja himself who threw the challenge at the general. Such was Ranjit's confidence that, one day, during the course of an evening with Ventura, while Lotus was dancing in front of them, Ranjit Singh commented on her attachment to him, categorically stating that no offers of advantage of affection from other quarters would sway her from her obsession with the maharaja.

'Well, the rest is history, as after several polite attempts on the part of Ventura to convince the maharaja, about the impropriety of his attempting to rival his sovereign, the challenge was accepted.'

'Bloody nymphomaniac she had become,' remarked Hari.

'And how would you know that? Maybe the maharaja had become impotent?'

'Incorrect! This is absurd and unfair. Absolutely wrong, sir! Why talk about the exploits of the maharaja just because he is dead? Look at the folks around us. At least he had consolidated the Sikh kingdom and did not let it get fragmented like the present lot, who at every step have compromised the interests of the state for the sake of votes.

'And talking about his harem, haven't we all read about a well-known senior member of one of our prominent political groups gyrating to DJs at parties? In fact, Shakespeare described Desdemona as very fair, yet suspect in fame. And to this day, from Venice to Verona, such matters may probably be the same.

'We all know about the dalliances of Dilraj Singh of a leading national party,' said Hari, rising to Ranjit Singh's defence.

The class was startled at this vehement defence.

'Osborne, you...' he thought to himself. 'Recording my bedroom exploits. What all have you been writing, one needs to find out. A scribe in the guise of a military-secretary? Were you, Osborne? One was always wary of your lot, the gori chamadis.'

'Apne Ranjit Singhji, zara thand rakho, thand (our very own Ranjit Singhji, be cool),' said a snide voice from within the class, as the bell signalled the end of the forty-five-minute history class.

'Thank you, sir,' said Hari, rather sheepishly, realising what an ass he had made of himself.

'But from where the fuck is all this information coming?' he wondered.

He desperately needed to talk to somebody and share this sudden turn of events. Taking out his new 3G iPhone from his pocket, he dialled a number. Obviously, he had no plans of sharing with Suzanne the previous week's encounter with Gaitri.

Two

Hard rock, heavy metal to be precise, was blaring from the speakers when Hari led Suzanne to the bar. The blasting sound of electric and bass guitars, keyboards, and drums pumped up the atmosphere. The bar was throbbing with life. Lava, at the Taj Chandigarh, had just about managed to get the formula right and had become the new happening place for clubbers. It was also quite the sniff bar with men and women on the prowl.

Though Hari would have preferred to spend time with Suzanne in the plush but muted Orchid Lounge, away from the prying eyes of Chandigarh's 'kakas', Suzanne had other ideas.

While Suzanne Sharma belonged to a conservative middle-class Brahmin family, she loved the Page 3 life and liked to be seen at all the fashionable places in the city. And at her date's expense. Not that she deliberately fished for rich dudes, but she just had a natural inclination towards them. Caste, creed, and religion were no barriers. All that mattered were money and looks. She had liked Hari the moment he had introduced himself to her on the train while taking the adjacent seat.

—⁂—

'I am Hari Sandhu,' he had said, his voice gruff from some wild partying the night before, sounding sexy enough for any girl to sit up and take notice. In addition, Hari's tall, athletic physique and good looks were fairly irresistible.

'Hi, I'm Suzanne, from Chandigarh,' the fair and tall girl with brown eyes and black hair had replied. 'You're quite unlike the majority of Chandigarh guys who would have fumbled for ways to introduce themselves.'

'Ha, never had to face that,' Hari had replied, quickly slipping fifty bucks into the steward's pocket, to keep up the regular inflow of beverages and snacks.

Typically, he would have dozed off if there'd been a stodgy babu or a neta by his side, but the beautiful girl on the window seat could not be left on her own. She needed company. And hell! What if he snored while sleeping, or unknowingly scratched his crotch, she would definitely have been put off.

He had learnt that she was a student of Government College for Girls in Sector 11 and was keen to become a psychologist.

—⁂—

Now at the bar, Suzanne sounded totally baffled, turning her lager mug around.

'So you're trying to tell me that you get fits of information and you don't know where all that comes from?'

'Yes,' replied Hari nodded.

'I've had a couple of embarrassing moments,' he added, regretting it the moment he said it. He knew Suzanne would ask for details.

'Like what?' asked Suzanne, who looked stunning in her black LBD and over-sized silver loops. The tantalising mole on her earlobe made things more exciting for Hari, who had a fetish for moles. However, this wasn't the moment for these thoughts; he had to hurry with an explanation. It was perfectly legitimate, but no way could he mention the previous week's incident about making love to A and screaming out B's name!

'It's funny how I have been blurting out information about the Sikh ruler Ranjit Singh without ever knowing anything about him. Today, in the history class, I said things which I have no clue about. In fact, it was the first ever class on Ranjit Singh.'

'And the second?' asked Suzanne getting interested in Hari's tale, ready to dig out answers from whatever little she could recall from her course books.

'Ummm... the second one, ummm... it was again in class when I recalled the names of two of Ranjit Singh's court dan... dan... dancers and one Englishman's name,' said Hari. 'Yeah, Osborne it was,' Hari's eyes wandered, unable to face Suzanne's piercing look.

'Nautch girls, you mean. Dude, what do you have in mind?' asked Suzanne, amused by Hari's confession, her first mug of beer making her a little chirpier.

'Two more Kingfishers, please,' said Hari to the bartender as he simultaneously waved at a couple of guys who were just entering the bar. 'Another one gone,' he thought to himself as he saw Jasjit Singh, his classmate from school, in his new clean-shaven avatar. Not that he had obeyed the diktat of the tenth Sikh guru to keep hair unshorn, but whenever a Sikh friend got his hair cut, Hari always felt disturbed, even though momentarily. He knew the exact reason why a teenager did that. For the girls, of course. In his case, it had been Sukhmani, who in spite of being Sikh herself, was averse to dating a 'surd'. Cut-surd she would prefer any day to the banias and the lalas. Terms that have emerged from public schools, 'cut-surd' is slang for a Sikh with shorn hair, while a 'surd' is one who has maintained the proper Sikh demeanour.

Hari's mother Jaspreet Kaur's pleas to her son to not cut his hair had fallen on deaf ears. Since after the days of terrorism in Punjab in the 1980s, an overwhelming number of Sikh youth succumbed to the misconception that cutting one's hair was a sure shot way of getting girls. This belief was further compounded by post 9/11 hate-crime incidents in the US, where the Sikhs were constantly mistaken for Arabs. Sikh youth from Punjab, who fancied an American dream, made a beeline for salons, a business that is now thriving in Punjab and its capital city Chandigarh – quite a change from a point of time in history when a Sikh scalp with unshorn hair carried a price. Ironically, it still does. Hari had paid a thousand bucks at *Headmasters* to get his long hair cut. In fact, the joke doing the rounds in the local government college was that an additional 'K' had been added to the customary five Ks of the Sikh religion (the five being kacha, kanga, kara, kesh, kirpan) – Kap. Sikh pride stabbed by its very own people!

'Beer,' said the steward placing two tumblers on the table.

'Thanks,' said Hari, as Suzanne sipped her beer, licking clean the froth off her lips with her tongue. Whether she had made her first move or not, Hari couldn't quite comprehend. He was still somewhat confused. Also, he didn't want to take any risk with Suzanne as the entire effort of wooing her shouldn't be lost because of one failed sexual attempt. He wanted to sort this out in his head before attempting to make love to a girl who would then give him pleasure for a longer time rather than stride out of the house in a huff, like Gaitri did.

'But you're Sikh, aren't you? So you must know something about Ranjit Singh?' asked Suzanne, as the music jumped between hard rock and rock 'n' roll. 'Whatever my little knowledge of psychology tells me, there must be a reason for this madness,' she said while moving herself provocatively to the music. 'Or you just might be overreacting.'

There's more to this madness, thought Hari. 'The only information I know about him is from my grandmother who would narrate tales of the gurus, Sikh warriors, and episodes from the *Ramayana* and *Mahabharata*. I remember her telling me that Ranjit was a born ruler, but nothing had come easy to him. I mean, he was a puny little fellow and actually got a wife to handle at the age of six, and Mehtab Kaur, his wife, was only five. And guess what, he obviously could not have sex with her. The "willy" wouldn't stand erect at that age, even if he ordered it to, in his capacity as a maharaja. You know what I mean?' he said, breaking into laughter over his own remark.

'That's one hell of a grandmother you must have had to tell you this,' Suzanne ribbed him and laughed out loud.

'Okay, chill,' said Hari, quickly coming to his grandmother's defence, imagining how Biji must have sounded while making such a remark. Marriages those days were marriages of convenience where two dynasties, misls in this case, through marriage, made enviable alliances, something that is still very much prevalent in Punjab. For example, Sangat Singh, who once headed the Akali party, got his daughter married to the grandson of a former chief minister, who headed the Congress – a party diametrically opposite to Sangat Singh's party in terms of ideology.

'Mehtab belonged to the Kanhaiya misl. But boy! What a mother-in-law Ranjit Singh had in Sada Kaur! Tough woman!

'Poor lad, caught in a tug-of-war between his mother Raj Kaur and mother-in-law Sada Kaur who were trying to get him under their influence. Ranjit, mostly to stay out of this shit, spent time annexing territories, away from the bickering of the argumentative women, "takrari" as he called them.

'What else do I remember of Dadi's stories? He was born on 13 November 1780, a Scorpio, at Gujranwala, and was struck by a virulent attack of small pox when he was six. His father, Maha Singh, who was then the headman of the Sukerchakia group of sardars, launched a mammoth prayer event across his entire territory. The boy survived, but he was blinded in one eye; and the virus pitted his face badly. Also, he obviously wasn't like the "spoilt brats" of today who grow with PSP or Nintendo Wii video games. No friggin' multiplexes for him. Most of his life was spent learning horse-riding, sword-fighting, swimming, wrestling, and hunting. He regularly attended religious services at the gurdwara and was educated about Sikh scriptures and values, something that he always kept in mind while in power. Damn! That one year at Bhagu Singh Dharamshala in Gujjaranwala was tough. Boring, couldn't last there for more than a year with all those numbers and other stuff. Perhaps impractical in that day and age where riding a horse or using the lance was akin to an MBA or an IIT degree.'

This was not the indifferent nineteen-year-old dude Hari speaking, thought Suzanne but decided against interrupting his train of thoughts even though she was clueless about whether Hari's blurtings were true. But one thing was certain – this was not grandma's bedroom tale being retold. Nor was it from *Amar Chitra Katha*. The very thought sent a chill down her spine.

'With the genes of Desan Budh Singh, who is said to have been baptised by the tenth guru, Guru Gobind Singh, himself, Ranjit Singh developed a personality unlike the Sikh leaders of today,' said Hari excitedly. 'Actually, Sikh leadership was at its lowest ebb when Ranjit came to power and it still is, even so many years after his death. Sahib Singh Bedi, a descendant of Guru Nanak, had conducted the coronation ceremony by daubing twenty-year-old Ranjit's forehead with saffron paste on Baisakhi in 1801, thus proclaiming him as the sarkar of Punjab. They say his strength of personal character and prudence is unparalleled, even two hundred years after his death. Ranjit was one of those that seemed destined to win his way to distinction and achieve greatness, in spite of being illiterate.

'Believe you me, sovereignty doesn't come easy. Like I said earlier, after his father's death at the young age of twenty-nine, Ranjit had ascended as the chief of the Sukerchakia misl through a simple ceremony called "pagri". Oh man! Was the atmosphere hostile! He was what, only ten, and surrounded by enemies, suspicious friends, jealous sardars and who not.

'A freebooter though, Budh Singh's tales of derring-do, especially about his feat of crossing rivers astride his piebald mare Desan, were much spoken about in early eighteenth century Punjab. Bahut daring tha, baba,' said Hari.

'Ranjit was named Budh Singh at birth, but his father, who was then out for the siege of Rasulnangar, on his return, quickly changed the infant's name to Ranjit which means "victor of battles". Also one of the drums of the tenth guru was named Ranjit. The entire community had broken into a frenzy, with celebrations and generous donations to the poor,' carried on Hari, recounting all this with immense excitement.

'Laudanum?' asked Hari.

'Sir?' said the waiter, taken aback by the order. He had never heard the word in spite of having worked in some real fancy bars.

'Oh, no nothing! Forget it! More beer, please,' said Hari, signalling at the empty beer glasses, trying to put a face to his order.

'Laudanum! What the heck is that?' asked Suzanne trying hard to hide her anxiety.

'It's an alcoholic herbal preparation of opium.'

'Holy shit! What the hell are you talking about? Are you on opium?' she asked, getting a bit worried about her night out with Hari.

He laughed. 'That's what Ranjit Singh liked, other than his special brandies which were fermented out of dried raisins and crushed pearls, especially when he was in his harem amongst the nautch girls. The poor Brits tried hard to make him drink port, claret, hock, champagne, etc., but scotch was the closest he got to the firang stuff. The brandies were prepared by a Hungarian homeopath… one Dr Martin Honigberger, the same dude who mixed his gunpowder.'

'You were crazy in your previous birth!' said Suzanne, realising the gravity of her statement even as she mouthed it.

However, before Hari could react, she placed her hand on his. 'Up for a dance?' she asked. At that moment, she wanted to break free from the intensity of the conversation. This was not what she had planned when Hari had asked her out for the evening. He had wanted to share something, but she hadn't quite anticipated that the events of the evening would unfold this way. He seemed like a reincarnation of some maharaja of Punjab about whom she had heard vaguely. Unbelievable!

The music had switched to a juggle between Punjabi pop and Bollywood. This was typical of bars in Chandigarh. A few large pegs, three at least, and everybody in Chandigarh likes to do the 'fixing-the-bulb movement', possible only on Punjabi music. In Bollywood, while training dancers for bhangra, it is common knowledge that choreographers explain the actions by saying 'fix the bulb and kick the dog'.

Still holding his hand, actually the tips of his fingers, Suzanne guided Hari to a tight corner where one could stand face-to-face and move a bit. The perfect way for couples who were getting to know each other better or warming up to the evening.

'Which school did you go to, Hari?' asked Suzanne

'St John's. And you?'

'Sacred Heart, your neighbouring school.'

'Sacred Heart was always the sisterly kind, I mean for us Johnians. We wooed girls from Carmel Convent.'

'Hmmm... anyhow I think it's time for you to drop me home,' said Suzanne, her smile naughty and the twinkle in her eyes saying, 'sure if you wanna drop me, drop me, baby'. Hari placed his hands on her slim waist as if to suggest 'no way'. Pulling her a step closer, he started guiding her, ignoring the fact that Mika's Punjabi number asked for brisker movements than just a sway. He saw her eyes close for a split second as his hands touched her waist. He was certain that she had liked the feel of his hands.

It was close to 11.30 p.m., the deadline beyond which excise laws of Chandigarh didn't allow alcohol to be served. That worked as a party pooper for the drinkers.

'No more beer, sir. The bar is now closed,' were words enough to piss off Hari, who stormed out, abusing Punjabi style. 'Maanchods', 'bhenchods', flew out unchecked, interrupted occasionally with their English equivalents.

'Motherfucking excise guys, my parties would last... and Mohran would dance and dance... even though she found me damn ugly,' said Hari as he pressed hard on the accelerator of his Ford Endeavour, a gift from his dad, a big landlord in Punjab. 'Yeah, god was busy distributing power to me, Mohran, that's why I'm ugly,' he screamed, drunk on beer.

'Oh god, not again,' murmured Suzanne. She was in no state to hear more about Ranjit Singh. Not after six mugs of strong beer. But suddenly, when they were nearing her house in Sector 33, her kinky side ceded. After all, she had drunk six mugs of Kingfisher.

'When you make love to me, you can imagine me as your Lily, Mohran or Subhu,' she said, rolling her tongue on her lips that were delicious enough to eat. 'I will not protest, Ranjit.

Bye,' she said, her beautiful body disappearing into the safety of her house. How she would handle her parents was not Hari's concern.

Three

With such a massive hangover, college was the last thing on Suzanne's mind when she woke up the next morning, still in the black dress that she had worn the previous night. Drunk as hell, she had collapsed on her bed and slept for straight ten hours. Her parents, Professor Devinder Sharma and his wife, were in Tirupati; the professor availing his leave travel concession. Her older sister, Radhika, was sleeping in her room, or having phone sex with her US-based fiancé who worked out of home as an investment banker.

Once up, Suzanne's mind just wouldn't digress from Hari despite the throbbing pain in her head. Though only their second meeting – technically their first if the chance train encounter was discounted – Hari had made quite an impression on her. What was it? Was it that she wanted to help him overcome the sudden change in his life? Or was it that she had a crush on him? Either way, her mind wouldn't let go of him, rewinding and forwarding from the time they had entered the bar till the moment he dropped her home.

'All friggin' Gaitri's fault,' she thought. Had Gaitri, her best friend, not narrated the events of her first sexual experience with Hari, Suzanne, even in her wildest dreams, would not have blurted what she did, 'When you make love to me, you can imagine me as your Lily, Mohran or Subhu. I will not protest, Ranjit.'

'Oh god, what must Hari be thinking,' she thought, burying her head into her knees. And as for knowing about Gaitri's encounter with Hari, she better keep this little secret to herself.

Hari had no intention of getting out of bed. College or no college. Astride galloping horses, turbaned lancers shouting 'Sat Sri Akal' were dominating his subconscious mind when his mother made the first call for breakfast at about 10:30 a.m. The faint call of 'Hari! Breakfast,' was overpowered by the shriller voice of a puny little Sikh shouting 'Chal Laili' to his mare while urging his forces to charge full throttle.

'Faujan agan vadho (Forces move forward)!' yelled the little sardar in his Pothwari accent, as he stood firmly on his stirrups, the horse charging at a full gallop towards a distant fort. The man's flowing beard was flying with the pace of the horse. 'Chal Laili!' yelled Ranjit in a full-throated voice, spurring his Kathiawari mare in her abdomen to gallop faster, the lancers and swordsmen following suit.

He knew that getting the indomitable Lahore fort would be a landmark step towards establishing the Sikh empire. He had been chosen to lead the charge by various Sikhs misls at a Sarbat Khalsa in Amritsar.

Amritsar. The very name suddenly evoked a divine feeling, as images of the Harmandir overtook battlefield scenes. These images became vivid as he now formulated a plan to annex the holy city. Founded by the fourth guru, Guru Ram Dass, the most important city for Sikhs – Amritsar would be his next target after capturing Lahore.

Shah Zaman, grandson of the Afghan plunderer Ahmad Shah Abdali, who had made Lahore his capital after seizing it from the Mughals in 1748, had been chased out of Amritsar in January 1797 by Ranjit Singh; but a formal annexation would be of utmost importance to establish an empire based on the temporal and spiritual doctrine of the Sikhs. An empire committed to secularism in its truest form, unlike the collapsing social fabric of modern-day India. No one in his empire would be permitted to get away with murdering or raping helpless women on the basis of caste and religion, Hari pledged, tossing around in an attempt to catch the cool blast of the air-conditioner.

For such a plan to successfully unfold, Lahore obviously was the first target and under any circumstances, he needed to conquer it. Being the largest city of Punjab, Lahore was the perfect place to set up the capital of the Khalsa Empire. Most importantly, it had all that was required of a capital. Located on the banks of the river Ravi, the city, in the two thousand years of its existence, had developed into a hub of learning as well as a centre of art and culture. Named Lavpura, after Lav, the elder son of Lord Rama, the big boost for Lahore had come in 1584, when the Mughal emperor Akbar had shifted his capital to this city.

Supremacy over Lahore would also arrest the constant sucking of wealth by various Muslim invaders and put an end to the era of oppression which had begun in the eleventh century when the then ruler of Ghazni, Mahmud Ghazni, had looted the Indian subcontinent seventeen times starting from AD 1001 and made Lahore the capital city for the first time. Ghazni's looting exercise – temples and monasteries being prime targets – had soon assumed political dimensions; and by AD 1027, he had established the Ghaznavid Empire, extending from the Caspian Sea to the river Yamuna in the Indian subcontinent. Ghazni's entry from the Khyber Pass had also laid a foundation for further plunderers and people with political ambition in Central Asia to follow his path after his death.

The residents of the city also favoured Ranjit, to the extent that a joint deputation comprising Muslims, Sikhs, and Hindus had secretly approached him to free them from the mismanagement and tyranny of three Sikh chieftains – Chet Singh, Sahib Singh, and Mohr Singh of the Bhangi misl, whose ancestors had partitioned Lahore and its surrounding areas into separate Berlin-like zones. Moreover, Ranjit had entered into a secret agreement with Zaman Shah (grandson of Ahmad Shah Abdali) in 1798 who had conceded Lahore to him; it was time to enforce his claim.

Operation Lahore took place on the tenth day of Muharram in the year 1799, and had barely lasted a couple of days. It was, in fact, an anti-climax to the feisty fighting style of Ranjit. The enemy in the fort, consisting of a few thousand men, had surrendered without a fight after Ranjit's forces had surrounded the city in the night while the town was celebrating Muharram. Though Ranjit would have typically wanted to storm the otherwise impenetrable fort to teach the men a lesson, his mother-in-law Sada Kaur, who had also reached with a sizeable army, had advised him against doing so.

'Ranjiteya, ehvien kahlaa na pey (Oh Ranjit, don't be in such a tearing hurry). The forces in the fort will surrender themselves as they are left with no option, thanks to lack of provisions,' she had argued belligerently.

'Mataji's advice cannot be ignored,' Ranjit had thought to himself, even though he was itching to wield his sword to get over with this expedition and visit the Shalimar Gardens with Suzanne. He had been celibate for almost three days.

Phew, thought Hari, springing out of his bed, his dream shattered at the very name... Suzanne. Her words from last night were ringing in his head, adding strength to his morning libido. 'When you make love to me, you can imagine me as your Lily, Mohran or Subhu.'

'How the heck did she know about those women?' he thought, reeling under the events that had taken place over the last one week.

Meanwhile, Suzanne, taking charge of her bearings, switched on her laptop and googled Dr Gilbert Brown.

'Dr Gilbert Brown, Psychiatrist, specializes in past life therapy, and lives in Los Angeles, California,' she read out aloud from his home page and clicked on the contact icon, seeking his e-mail id.

Four

Dear Dr Brown,

I am a twenty-one-year-old girl from India, seeking your help. My nineteen-year-old boyfriend has been blurting out information that surely has not been acquired in this lifetime. He has been talking about the life of a former king from Punjab, a state located in North India.

Though there are no signs of him being disturbed or odd behaviour, he divulged unexpected information in his history class and during a date with me. The same also happened when he was having sex with his former girlfriend. While making love, he imagined her as one from his harem. How do you explain this?

Doctor, I want to help him. Is he a reincarnation of that king? Please help, I love him.

I am a student of psychology and will therefore be able to

understand the reason behind this kind of behaviour if you
could guide me.

Best regards,
Suzanne
Chandigarh, India

A couple of days later...

Barring the exchange of a few text messages, it had been two
days since Suzanne and Hari had met or spoken to each other.
Suzanne, embarrassed by what she had said while parting, had
just wanted to lie low.

On Monday afternoon, Hari was driving his father to their
native village in Jalandhar district. Hari's father, Shamsher Singh,
didn't foresee much of a professional career for his son. Had
there been any inclination towards serious education, thought
Shamsher, Hari would have opted for the medical or non-medical
stream while seeking admission in eleventh standard. History,
sociology, and public administration were not the subjects that
took one far professionally. At least that is what Shamsher firmly
believed. And most certainly not by whiling away time at pubs
and parties.

Realising that managing family properties would be the
career that Hari would most likely end up adopting, Shamsher
Singh insisted that Hari accompany him on every visit to the
village. It was better to expose them young even at the cost of
missing college. After all, the market value of his estate stood
at over rupees one hundred crore, and maintaining a property

worth that much was more than a full time job and a skill that no college could teach you. He himself had learnt it the hard way after his father, Sardar Jagjodh Singh, had passed away at a young age, leaving Shamsher to handle the vast estate on his own. Through years of experience, Shamsher had perfected the art of managing it all – from battling family intrigues, to handling the bureaucracy, the local patwari and thanedar, and the egoistic and greedy politician ... Shamsher had become a pro. He now wanted Hari to understand and grasp the nuances as that was an integral part of managing property affairs in India.

'Dad, could we make a quick stop at Sector 17? Just want to pick up a few books from Capital,' said Hari as they drove out of the driveway of their house in his father's newly acquired 5 Series BMW. It was a Monday morning. Reading books was something Shamsher always encouraged. An ardent reader himself, the tall bulky sardar in his late forties nodded his head in approval, pleased with Hari's proposal.

'Pick up Osho's translation of the *Japji Sahib* for me,' said Shamsher, handing out a one thousand rupee note to Hari as Hari unlocked his seatbelt.

'He has a book on *Japji Sahib* too?' asked Hari with a surprised look on his face. Just the other day he had seen his father reading one titled *From Sex to Super Consciousness*.

'If it pours heavily, no point in wasting time watching television. In any case, news channels are crap. I prefer reading,' replied Shamsher, wondering what other books he might have sitting on his tiny book-rack at the farm.

'Visiting Amritsar to offer prayers at the Golden Temple is also not a bad option if the rain interrupts farm operations,' thought Shamsher as Hari ran to the book store.

Though proud of siring two sons, a very typical Punjabi trait, Shamsher constantly worried about Hari's future. The loss of Neil, his younger son, in a car crash a year-and-a-half ago had shattered him and his wife, Jaspreet. The tragedy had also left an indelible mark on Hari's mind. He had been in the navigator seat and seen his brother die in front of his eyes, while he escaped without getting even a single scratch on his body. Life had departed into oblivion much before the emergency services could reach his brother, who was dead cold right next to him within seconds of the crash. The open airbags were no consolation.

'Injustice, Dad,' Hari had wept over the phone while informing his father that they had lost Neil to an American motorway. The boys had hit a Coca Cola trailer from the rear, on Pacific Coast Highway (101), while driving from San Francisco to San Diego in the summer of 2007 during a vacation. The shock had been so enormous that the otherwise outgoing Hari had virtually become a recluse, till the parents, gathering courage, took him to a psychiatrist for help. All this was done under wraps, of course. The professional help did wonders and Hari was able to come to terms with the tragedy, and was almost back to his old self within a couple of months.

'Shamsher, you are a lucky guy. Hari has come out unscathed, twice,' the doctor had said as he gave a clean chit to Hari. The immediate step Shamsher had taken after Hari's recovery was buying him an SUV with airbags, to ensure greater safety for his surviving son. Rest, he had left on Wahe Guru resulting in frequent trips to Amritsar and the Golden Temple.

Ranjit Singh: Maharaja of Punjab by eminent Sikh historian Khushwant Singh, and *Lion of the Punjab: A Diary Account of*

Ranjit Singh's Time by Captain Osborne attracted Hari's attention immediately.

'What an ugly man you were, Ranjit. You look like a mouse,' said Hari to himself as he looked at the cover of both the books that carried Ranjit Singh's pictures. 'Mohran wasn't wrong after all,' he thought as he walked to the sales counter to pay the bill. What he didn't notice was the girl entering the book store and also asking for a biography of Ranjit Singh.

'Should I put all the books into one bag?' asked the salesman pointing at the two volumes of *True Name* by Bhagwan Rajneesh.

'No, separately please,' replied Hari.

He had no idea why he wanted to hide Ranjit Singh from his family. He also had no idea why he wanted to buy his biographies, especially if he himself was well versed about the maharaja's life. Maybe, it was the only way to get some concrete information on the details of his life.

The lion would get to read his own tale.

Five

Suzanne was pleasantly surprised to hear from Dr Gilbert Brown within a couple of days. As an authority on past life therapy and an author of many bestsellers, the head of the psychiatry department of Mind Clinic & Hospital, Los Angeles, Dr Brown was familiar with India. Not because the word 'India' from the late twentieth century onwards had become an irritant to a handful of political honchos, ill advised about India's progress, but because the doctor had always been fascinated with India's rich heritage. Its spirituality and the Hindu re-birth theory had a special place in his heart, though he wasn't sure whether karma was a key to determine one's rebirth.

Suzanne's e-mail had immediately attracted his attention and he had made it a point to respond to the young lady as soon as possible.

Hi Suzanne,

It is indeed a pleasure to write to you. I read your e-mail and was immediately drawn towards it. I have a special affinity for India, given its mythology, kings, and modern-day progress.

Regarding your query, I must mention that there is a reason for everything that occurs. When it does, we usually do not have the insight to realize the cause, but with time and patience, we can bring it to light. I am keen to help you but you might want to regress him on your own. However, I must warn you – it could change his, and your life permanently.

We could fix a time and date and I would be glad to offer help via a live video conference and ask your friend about his harem. Seems like we have a crazy maharaja on our hands!

Warm regards,
Dr Gilbert Brown

After returning from college, Suzanne would usually check her emails. Her routine involved leaving home at approximately eight-thirty to reach in time for her psychology class at nine.

Mrs Bhatia did not like her students to arrive late for class, not even by a minute; so Suzanne's morning drill was always rushed. Once in college, the mundane would take over, of jostling from one classroom to the other. The forty-five minute break would usually be spent with Gaitri, who was a year younger to Suzanne. Today, she would have to find an excuse to not meet her. Suzanne's crush on Hari was intensifying with each passing minute and Gaitri was the last person she could confide in about this.

After reading Dr Brown's email, Suzanne had immediately wanted to speak to Hari. But something stopped her from calling him. She couldn't possibly address him as Ranjit Singh as he had not even asked for her help. She didn't really want to jump the gun. And mouthing rubbish after gulping six beers was an excuse even the most promiscuous girl could get away with. At that moment, she was in her full senses and no way was she calling Hari to tell him what she had been up to.

Maybe another beer date was what was required, she thought, to decide. This time she would surely opt for Orchid Lounge, she thought, amazed at how an attraction could disconnect one from the rest of the world. It made her feel content for the first time in her life, even though for her, it still remained a mystery whether Hari felt the same way about her.

'Back off, sister,' she said to herself. They'd barely met a couple of times and love was a word too much into the future.

Her reply to Dr Brown's email would have to wait till next week she thought as she replayed a recently downloaded song on her laptop, half a smile forming on her face. *All I think about, is you* played from the tiny speakers of her notebook while she scurried to the kitchen to get herself a coffee. It was four and she was desperate for her evening dose of caffeine.

Hari must have been cruising at about ninety kilometres per hour – a higher speed not possible given the enormity of indiscipline shown by commuters on the Chandigarh-Ropar highway – when they reached Ropar. The Tulip Resort on the southern bank of the river Sutlej was a must-stop for Shamsher. The beautiful gurdwara, Taapistan (originally Tibbi Sahib), that stood on a small hillock on the opposite bank was a mesmerising sight for even an atheist. The mellow flow of the Sutlej – mellow because it had been barraged barely a few metres away to divert water to the canal network that fed the irrigation needs of the desert state of Rajasthan – always rejuvenated Shamsher.

A Diet Coke from the kiosk located outside the ramshackle restaurant and a gentle bow of the head, face towards the gurdwara, was a ritual Shamsher Singh had been following for years. Hari, who had started accompanying his father more recently, had by now become familiar with his father's routine and the place itself.

However, on this particular occasion and for no apparent reason, Hari had started feeling somewhat uneasy the moment the tyres of his finely tuned German machine rolled over the first span of the bridge on river Sutlej. Spasms in the belly apart, bewildering imagery suddenly replaced the regular din of Indian roads.

The approaching overloaded Tata truck suddenly looked like an elephant.

A bus that was screaming hard to overtake the truck on the bridge looked like a camel, neck sticking out, as the camel jockey tried all tricks in his quiver to get past the mammoth elephant. The yellow protruding radiator of the orange truck looked like the trunk of a giant elephant, which apparently seemed to enjoy its walk on the bridge, not giving two hoots to the camel's loud snort and in no mood to budge from its established position. Dotted with fancy jewels and precious stones, the gajraj was basking in the glory of being the maharaja's ride. The maharaja was mounted atop the tusker in a golden howdah, his right hand on his golden scabbard inlaid with gems, and the other twirling his moustache.

As if this sudden commotion was not enough, the sound of the engine of a passing SUV rattled Hari's ears. It sounded like the canter of a hundred horses piloting the maharaja's ride. The scene was now stirring up unbearable pain in the boy's innards.

In order to cross the bridge quickly, Hari pushed his foot on the accelerator further, but the over speeding only added to his misery. 'Phatak-phatak' went the BMW on the pot holes.

'Laili, holi hoja!' shouted Hari trying to pacify the speeding BMW. He would do the same with Laili, his mare, who had once taken off when his troops had given him a gun salute after one of his victories.

'Brake maar, khoteya (brake, you donkey)!' shouted Shamsher, as he saw the fiery-coloured truck racing towards them, trumpeting, urging the lesser beast to either get out of its way or be crushed. Two screeching sounds were heard moments after Shamsher made those warning shouts, the driver of the truck and Hari braking just in time to avoid what could have been a deathly collision.

'Shukar hai Wahe Guru da (thank you, Almighty), you are okay,' said Shamsher looking at Hari with eyes full of relief, and then immediately turned his head towards the gurdwara to bow for the second time.

Hari would have noticed the tears in his father's eyes had he not immediately rushed out of the car, gunning for the truck driver who had dared to come in the way of the raja's sawari. Was it road rage or a rush of teenage blood mixed with those rare occasions when the maharaja lost his cool that led to a verbal fight on the narrow bridge? Nobody knew. However,

Hari's vocabulary of Punjabi abuses was up to the mark, from Shamsher's point of view. He was a practical father. In fact, 'Bhen da lalna' was a new one for Shamsher, and he had no idea what it meant. But it sounded good, so he would use it the next time he had to abuse his lazy labourers.

While 'bhenchods' and 'maanchods' rent the air, drowning the blare of horns from irate commuters, who had lined up on either side of the blockade, something stopped Hari from ordering the policeman on duty to lash the butt of the offender twenty-five times. 'Ehde chhitran te pachi kore maro (spank his bums),' he wanted to tell the man in khaki.

What pulled Hari back confused him – a voice from within suggested he treat his subjects with care and love.

'This is getting bad,' he thought to himself as he quietly slipped back into the car ignoring the truck driver's challenge to sort out the mess. 'Je maan da doodh peeta hai te aaja (if you have had your mother's milk, come and fight)!' shouted the driver from his seat, by now rolling his sleeves to take on the young fellow.

Promptly shuffling two gears, a reverse followed by a forward, Hari zipped his car across the bridge into the safe havens of the north of the Sutlej in less than forty seconds. The south of the Sutlej suddenly seemed alien; even for that matter Chandigarh, the town where he was born and brought up. Why did the peaks of the lower Shivaliks, with their bushy vegetation, seem so much more familiar and the river so different than its usual boisterous self? After all, the tide of the river was an important factor while deciding troop movements. Monsoons being a complete no-no. No king, no matter how invincible, could dare take on the mighty rivers of Punjab during the monsoons. But the Sutlej seemed so impotent now even though the monsoons had been great this year, the best Hari had seen. However, this particular monsoon was not even a patch on the ones witnessed in the eighteenth or nineteenth centuries. But then, the Sutlej had other reasons to become a nullah than mere lack of rainfall. The diversion of the river to canals, barraging at various points, population and urban explosion, and most importantly, depleting glaciers were factors that had turned the river into a virtual stream. Also, reports were pouring in that China was damming the river at the very source, the origin of Sutlej being somewhere in south-western China in the Tibetan plateau.

'When was this bridge constructed?' asked Hari surprised at this new development, as the car gained stability after crossing the bridge.

'In 1956 perhaps,' replied Shamsher, totally oblivious to the origin of the question. 'Did you not see the truck?' he asked sternly. 'And who is Laili? Is she one of your girlfriends?' added Shamsher in the same breath, bewildered by Hari's sudden loss of concentration.

'Yes,' replied Hari to both the questions. Though his answer to the first question was partially correct, Laili was in no way his girlfriend. It was a separate matter that he loved Laili more than the twenty odd wives and dancing girls from his harem. Having his 'feet in stirrups' early in the morning gave much more joy than a thousand orgasms combined together.

Only he knew what all he had to undergo to get the grey, sixteen-hands-tall Laili from the Barakzai brothers – Dost and Yar

Mohammad. And how many lies that bugger Yar Mohammad had cooked up to keep Laili! 'Chhitar marke laini payi (had to get it by force)'... since they came from that geographical area where only force worked as a convincing agent!

That too, from his other brother Sultan Muhammad after two years, the battle to acquire Laili starting in 1828 and ending in 1830.

Yar Mohammad who was the governor of Peshawar had refused to give the Persian mare as part of a tribute in spite of Ranjit's specific instructions to his foreign minister, Fakir Azizudin, to get it. Yar Mohammad had lied to Fakir Sahib saying that the mare was not in his possession. Intelligence officers, however, soon informed Ranjit Singh that Laili was indeed alive and in Yar's possession. After negotiations failed, an army under Budh Singh Sandhawalia was sent to get Laili as well as dispel the growing trouble with the tribesmen whom Yar was supporting.

'Ehdi aisi di taisi, haramzade di (he better give it, bastard)!' Ranjit had exclaimed, pacing up and down in his study with Budh Singh, while ordering the warrior to bring back the mare.

'Leke aiye ghori (better get the mare),' he had told Budh Singh. Unfortunately, Budh Singh Sandhawalia was killed in the fierce battle. It was thus left to his foreign generals, Allard and Ventura, who were fighting alongside Budh Singh to get Laili. However, in a classic twist to the tale, they were told that Laili was dead. Familiar with their master's temper, the generals, in another bid to get Laili this time, took Yar Mohammad's brother as hostage. This, too, yielded no result. Dissatisfied with the actions of the generals, the maharaja summoned his son Kharak Singh (the name suddenly evoking a strange feeling in Hari), and asked him to take an additional army to Peshawar to get

Laili by whatever means – money, force or even deposition of Yar Mohammad. But, things were to take a different course. Yar Mohammad was killed by the tribesmen and his brother Sultan Mohammad had fled the scene. It was only in 1830 when Sultan Mohammad was installed as governor in his brother's place by Prince Sher Singh and Ventura that he was asked to hand over Laili. He also dilly-dallied, and Ventura, who had become tired of this nonsense, arrested Sultan. Finally, Sultan had no choice but to give up the horse. History would observe that no horse since the Trojan Horse has ever been the cause of so much trouble and the death of so many brave men. The entire expedition cost nearly sixty lakh rupees and led to the loss of almost 12,000 soldiers.

Suddenly, Hari's father's BMW seemed a pittance in the entire scheme of things. Just at that moment, a convoy crossed them at breakneck speed near Balachaur, a small town just off the canal road. Four Land Cruisers and countless police pilot jeeps with security waving their hands frantically, zipped past them, urging commuters to get out of the way or be ready to be beaten up or even shot.

'Who is he?' Shamsher wondered about the VIP in the convoy. His father's voice transported Hari back to reality. This was the Punjab of today – modern and modified to a state where power, power broking, deceit, and corruption flourished. So said the media. What had increasingly disappeared from the minds of the rulers since the last two centuries was the welfare of the subjects, the so-called leaders treating the resources of the state as part of personal wealth. Two hundred years ago, even if the territories had been taken by force and plundering was one of the ways of tax collection, the king had the welfare of the subjects at heart. But the present five-year formula had rendered each ruler a plunderer of the level of a Ghazni or an Abdali. The organised state was nothing but a garb for personal fiefdom. National security was now the job of the Central Government. Corruption, a sophisticated version of plundering, had become the focus area of Punjab's polity. The Green Revolution of the 1960s had brought all-round progress, but had, at the same time, provided ample fodder to fill the coffers of the politicians.

Guilty of being untruthful to his father, Hari, for a moment, thought of sharing with him his current condition, but something stopped him. He did not want to weigh his father down again as the family had already gone through the trauma of his younger brother's death which was followed by Hari trying to cope with life without his brother. Though Hari was confident that his father would help him get out of this situation, just as he had brought him on an even keel the last time around, a voice within him urged him to handle this on his own. However, the question was – what was all this leading to?

Six

Tuesday, 9 September

It was exactly thirty hours since Hari had been in the village.

If the Sutlej bridge incident was the latest reckoner, Hari, who lay in bed, was definitely feeling concerned. For the second time, he seriously contemplated on whether he was actually a reincarnation of Ranjit Singh.

'Bloody hell,' he muttered, perturbed by the recent events. Though initially amusing, these unabated incidents – Gaitri storming out of his room, the conversation with his history professor, and the near car crash – had suddenly shaken the ground beneath his feet, though he was trying hard to comfort himself by thinking that god had chosen him to be the reincarnation of a maharaja.

'Am I, am I not?' he wondered yet again, feeling distinctively uneasy.

He felt an urgent need to speak to someone he could connect with. He was feeling very bogged down, especially since his father had made him spend the entire day getting introduced to all the local arthiyas (commission agents) and bank managers. Fat ones, dark ones, short ones with oiled hair, tall ones with centre partings and a comb in the back-pocket – he met them all.

His protests fell on deaf ears because his father thought it was prudent to meet them if the lad had to make any progress!

'Eh mera puttar (he is my son), Hari,' Shamsher would introduce him, depending on the English-speaking and understanding ability of the man in question.

Bansal saab was a case in point. He was the owner of 'Bansal Commission Agent' in Hoshiarpur town. Mr Bansal, after being introduced to Hari, started sermonising to the young boy on how lucky he was to have been born in Shamsher Singh's household. Sitting cross-legged on a mattress with a white sheet spread on it, his pot-belly seeking support from his knees, Bansal, while eulogising his family, said, 'Kakaji, boht lucky o tusaan, ke Shamsher bhaisahib de ghar paida hoye hoe (son, you are very lucky to have been born in Shamsher Singh's house).' 'Very nice man, very nice man,' he added as he tried to unwind his legs from their present position.

'What a sucker,' thought Hari. 'Friggin' fraud,' he said to himself, vividly remembering reading in a magazine about how commission agents exploit the poor and the marginalised farmers by charging them interest rates of forty-two percent and more. Because of the never-ending formalities to acquire a loan from the bank, the illiterate farmer usually ends up at the doorstep of these commission agents with folded hands, pleading for money, with a promise to sell his produce to only him.

In hindsight, the bania hadn't evolved one bit. His sinister designs were well concealed behind the garish, calendar art pictures of various gods that hung on the walls. Goddess Laxmi for unlimited wealth; Lord Shiva for an enhanced libido; Lord Sri Ram to showcase commitment to religion; and Guru Nanak to attract farmers, as most of them happened to be Sikhs. The maharaja's pictures had been replaced by Gandhi's, Nehru's or the chief minister's – all this to appease people belonging to different faiths and, of course, the leading political parties.

What had also not changed, in spite of the advent of fancy chairs, was how the bania sat in his shop. Not that the maharaja had never sat cross-legged, but he would sit in that manner only when he was in his durbar or dancing hall, drowning himself in laudanum, watching Mohran dance.

'Thoda thanda taan, sardar sahib, chalega (a little cold drink will do),' said Bansal, immediately calling his servant. 'Gian, doe Limke phadi (Gian, get two bottles of Limca),' he ordered the little Bihari boy.

'Cold hovey,' he added, raising his arm as if 'cold' was a code word, meant for very special guests. Come to think of it, yes! Given the dismal power situation in modern Punjab, the majority of the shopkeepers served soft drinks at room temperature because the deep freezers rarely functioned!

The arm action also gave Bansal an opportunity to scratch his hairy, heavily talcum-powdered yet sweaty armpit with his long nails, which had been grown for more effective itching. There was one stark difference between the bania and the guy in the Punjab police. While the bania concentrated on itching his armpits, stomach, and everywhere above the pelvic area, the latter's hands usually dived for the crotch for incessant itching and adjustment.

Eleven in the night was not exactly the time to imagine a Bansal scratch his armpit or a cop, his crotch. The wiser thing would be to fantasise about some hot chick, a bedtime ritual which he had been practising for the past four years before getting a chance to do the real thing with Gaitri.

With his left hand in his boxer shorts, his mind quickly retraced to last week's date with Suzanne. Shedding all inhibitions about calling her so late in the night, Hari hurriedly pulled out his iPhone from its charger with his right hand and dialled her number.

Suzanne, who had just got into bed and was flipping the pages of Patwant Singh and Jyoti M. Rai's biography of Ranjit Singh, was stumped to see Hari's name beeping on her mobile. It wasn't the lateness of the hour – as she herself had been eager to speak to him – but the sheer coincidence that freaked her out.

'Hari, are you okay?' was her first question, the extra concern somehow acting as a deterrent to Hari's growing libido as he had called her only for some good old dirty talk.

'Yes, honey,' he replied. For Hari, Suzanne was merely an object of lust.

Though Suzanne had developed a major crush on him, she was sure she would surrender only at an appropriate time. After all, Hari was no maharaja and couldn't force himself on her. So what if he was one in his previous life? And that, too, was yet to be established... if only everything went as per her plan of regressing him.

'Where are you?' she asked, her soft and gentle voice doing no good to Hari's mood.

'If I say Chandigarh, will you join me for a drive?' he asked, trying to divert Suzanne's attention from merely exchanging pleasantries to a more meaningful conversation.

'Not tonight,' replied Suzanne, playing hard to get, which in certain ways was also a cover up for last Friday's unabashed display of her desires.

'I'm in bed and reading this very exciting book,' she said, her voice virtually pleading Hari to probe further.

'Erotica?' asked Hari. 'I have some of the steamiest stuff in my library,' he continued, making yet another attempt to seduce the girl into a sex chat.

'Keep it for a rainy day,' replied Suzanne curtly, determined not to get lured by his overtures. She knew exactly what he had in mind. Besides, the Sharma household couldn't handle two women with their hands in their panties simultaneously. She had heard her sister's mobile ring only a few minutes ago and she was sure it was her fiancé. This Sharma household was supposed to be extremely conservative. *Hari Om, Hari Om!*

Lamenting her outburst on Friday night for the umpteenth time, Suzanne tried to keep the conversation about the book alive, 'It's a bio on Ranjit Singh.'

'I am reading what a naughty guy you were,' she said, her voice now changing its tone. Of course she did not tell him that the very first pages she read through were about Ranjit's harem.

'Good night, Hari, sleep tight,' she said, disconnecting the line and thus leaving him high and dry for the second time in a row.

'Bitch!' muttered Hari under his breath, his mind now rushing to seek an alternate fantasy girl to curtail his growing libido. Rajni, the village nambardar Tilak Raj's daughter, was also hot, thought Hari. In fact, she had scribbled her mobile number for him on a scrap of paper and slipped it into his hand. However,

Rajni was saved the trauma of becoming Hari's mere fantasy by a sharp beep on Hari's mobile.

'Hari, I think I like you. We need to meet soon. XXX Suzanne. Goodnight and don't be naughty,' read the text message.

—⟨◎⟩—

Propped up on her bed, Suzanne read on...

On the borderline between Ranjit Singh's harem and his court, between his private and his public life, there was a no man's land, a land of wine, song and dance. It was here that he used to spend his hours of relaxation – an evening once or twice... – Fakir Syed Waheeduddin.

'Let's see you woo me,' said Suzanne to herself as she read through the *Empire of the Sikhs*. The chapter titled 'The Unabashed Sensualist' had immediately drawn her attention as she tried to conjure up images of Subhu and Lily and other women, if any.

No less impressive than Ranjit Singh's achievements as an empire builder were his amatory exploits. The joys of dalliance with seductive, striking-looking women, doubtless, gave Ranjit the same pleasure as his conquests on the battlefield did.

Whatever the reason, he exulted in their company, viewing them as cherished trophies won in more intimate encounters. If a temptress caught his fancy, he was perfectly willing to be tempted.

'The dude doesn't seem to have changed one bit,' thought Suzanne, as she hunted for references that might help her when she would regress Hari into his past life. The two paragraphs that she had read convinced Suzanne that if the just concluded phone conversation had taken place back in Ranjit Singh's time, no way could she have refused his desire to have phone sex… that is if phones had existed then. For all you know, she might even have been in bed with him, if the maharaja was in the mood. How could anyone dare refuse a maharaja?

'He savoured the joys of sex with those who appealed to him, and made clear to courtiers, visitors, and his populace that he regarded the delight he got out of his beautiful consorts as his personal right.'

Seven

*H*aving pleasured himself, fantasising about Suzanne, Hari rushed to bring to bed the two books that he had bought the previous day. He flipped through *Maharaja of the Punjab*. He decided to read parts of the introduction first, though, like Suzanne, he was tempted to read about the maharaja's harem.

Ranjit has been poorly served by his biographers. Hindu and Sikh admirers deified him as a virtuous man and a selfless patriot. The academic apotheosis reduced a full-blooded man and an astute politician to an anaemic saint and a simple-minded nationalist. Muslim historians were unduly harsh in describing him as an avaricious freebooter. English writers, who took their material largely from Muslim sources, portrayed him as a cunning man (the cliché often used is 'wily oriental') devoid of moral considerations, whose only redeeming feature was his friendship with the British. They were not only not averse to picking up any gossip they could get their hands on (every oriental court has always been a whispering gallery of rumours), but also gave them currency by incorporating them in works of history. In recent years, monographs on different aspects of Ranjit Singh's government have been produced under the auspices of various departments of history in Indian universities. These are mostly catalogues to explain known facts put in chronological order without any attempt to explain them in terms of historical movements. This method of treatment makes the meteoric rise of Ranjit Singh and the equally meteoric collapse of his kingdom appear as freaks of history instead of a culmination of an important historical movement.

'Spot on,' muttered Hari to himself. All historical events had a reason, whether hidden or obvious. Though the history depends on how historians, biographers, and people view it, it still is, to quite an extent, unchangeable.

If the Sikhs had botched up and destroyed what he had established, it was completely their fault. Just because historians had the benefit of hindsight, which afforded them to write with a twenty-by-twenty vision, his actions could not be held against him. Rather, all through his rule, he had been sure that after his death, his successors, because of their ineptitude, would not be able to hold on to his empire and the entire land would eventually come under British control. That it would turn red (under British control) within a span of ten years was, however, something he hadn't fathomed. The Law of Entropy enveloped the Sikhs much quicker than he had anticipated. It was also aided by the infighting and treachery within their set-up.

Secondly, just because he happened to be the only Sikh king, his rise to power could not be construed a fluke – almost forty years of efficient rule was no fluke. Free India was just sixty years old. If this was the thumb rule, then his rule was as much a coincidence as India's freedom, which was an outcome of the Second World War, where the British became weak and maintaining colonies became unviable, some would argue.

In all sincerity, there was no design per se, to establish the kingdom that came about. But yes, the ambition to rule over a vast area of land was always there; the appetite whetted ever since Ranjit took charge of his misl at the age of eleven.

But the leaders of Bhangi, Nakkai, Ahluwalia, and Kanhaya misls were ambitions too.

In 1798, the map of Punjab was a jigsaw puzzle, ruled by different misls. A few areas such as Kasur, were ruled by a Pathan family, and Hansi in the south-east had become part of British adventurer George Thomas's kingdom. The Afghans still thought that most of northern India was theirs, and Shah Zaman, Ahmad Shah Abdali's grandson, was always on the lookout for opportunities to plunder. Given the circumstances, the situation, like English weather, would change every day, with each one conniving to annihilate the other. However, hidden behind this labyrinth was a situation simple enough for everyone to take advantage of. Any fellow with pluck and aplomb could just about establish an empire as big as Ranjit's.

Ranjit's simple tactic had been to keep his eyes and ears open and deal with each situation with a hands-on approach while remaining fully conscious of his strengths and weaknesses. This quality held him in good stead till his last days in dealing with the Sikhs, the British, and the Afghans.

Having said that, whatever tract of land came under his rule, he made sure it was secular, united, and governed with an iron hand, so as not to let criminal nobility take over the lives of the people. The tenth Sikh guru, Guru Gobind Singh, had dreamt of a Sikh commonwealth, whereby every individual – his religion, caste, and creed being of no consequence – could exist freely, without the fear of the radicals. Ranjit had to fulfill his guru's vision.

In spite of being born into a Sikh family, Ranjit joined Muslims and Hindus on numerous occasions in their prayers and visited Mecca and many Hindu teerths. Almighty had probably willed it that way. The smallpox attack that blinded him in one eye was perhaps His way of instructing Ranjit to see all religions as one. In fact, few of his earlier orders to his home minister, Fakir Nurrudin Sahib, after capturing Lahore vindicated his position.

Fakir Nuruddin Ji, may you be happy.

It is hereby decreed by His Highness with the utmost emphasis that no person in the city should practice highhandedness and oppression on the people. Indeed, if even His Highness himself should issue an inappropriate order against any resident of Lahore, it should be clearly brought to the notice of His Highness so that it may be amended. Protector of Bravery, Malwa Singh, should always be advised to dispense justice in accordance with legitimate right and without the slightest oppression and, furthermore, he should be advised to pass orders in consultation with the Panches and judges of the city and in accordance with the Shastras and the Quran, as pertinent to the faith of the parties, for such is our pleasure. And should any person fail to act in accordance with your advice or instructions, you should send him a formal letter so that it may serve as a proof on the strength of which His Highness may punish him for disobedience. It should be done in a way it is in the original.

Despatched from the court of Maharaja Ranjit Singh 31 Bhadon, 1882 Sambat.

– *The Real Ranjit Singh* by Fakir Syed Waheedudin

'Phew! *Bhadon* and *Sambat?* What are these?' Hari thought out loud. He made a mental note to check with his father though he knew it had something to do with the desi calendar.

There were no lengthy compendiums; yet by the standards of his time, his country was much more orderly and peaceful than modern India hoped to be. Oh come on, thought Hari. Even though so many wars were being fought all around by his forces, there was hardly any civil disorder in his empire. Perhaps his jutti (shoe) alone was able to achieve what numerous rules and regulations had failed to. Modern India, despite having a lengthy Indian penal code, could be held to ransom by just some rabble-rousers, who simply had the power to collect a few goons at short notice.

'Would they have dared in my... err... Ranjit Singh's time?' he thought. Five minutes was what it took for the longest trial to close in the Lahore Court, the king himself being the accuser, judge, and jury.

Anyone can steer a ship in calm seas, but only a master can navigate in a gale. Terrorism, financial crisis, ethnic violence, and poverty were storms India had to navigate through, but it seemed the captains were not fully equipped and trained to handle all situations simultaneously. Because they lived in constant self-denial, not wanting to let go of vote politics, which blurred their vision from recognising forces that were destabilising the country.

As for his fondness for wine and women, it was natural. In his life, he had discovered that the only way to resist them was to yield to them. However, he was not Rudyard Kipling's prototype of a maharaja, 'God created Maharajas so that mankind could have a spectacle of jewels and marble palaces.' He was a leader of the masses, a warrior; his weakness for gems was just a by-product of his position.

Hari had no clue when he fell asleep, reminiscing about the events of the last two centuries. His effort to catch up on some interesting bits failed to get beyond a few paragraphs. The intrigues, the treachery, and the betrayals that took place, especially after his death in 1839, were still to be read.

It was past midnight and Suzanne was unable to sleep. She made herself some coffee, intending to be up late to read what lay under the surface of Ranjit Singh's story before she could actually apply past life therapy on Hari. She wondered what sort of a regression it would be. Her protagonist was partially aware of his past life, though he did not fully believe that these flashes of information were because he was Ranjit Singh in his past life. Would this drill help Hari resume a normal life? She had read somewhere that past life memories can sometimes be causative factors of phobias, anxiety, and panic attacks but could be treated through hypnosis. Hari didn't seem to have symptoms of any of those, but he could end up being a wreck if these visions continued. The problem had to be nipped in the bud, she thought, as she clenched her fists; she had begun feeling slightly uncomfortable about the whole situation.

'I like the guy,' she thought assuring herself that what she had planned for Hari was in his best interests. She was convinced that hypnosis was the only way to help him get rid of these abrupt past life experiences. Many universities abroad, she had read, were conducting studies in parapsychology and had made huge strides in dealing with people having experiences like Hari's. In India, too, past life regression was fast becoming a popular practice and of course, there are many instances, down the ages, of traditional Indian healers practising it.

'Wow,' she said to herself, feeling overwhelmed. And then, with a slight smile, she turned her gaze to the book she was reading. Life surely was changing rapidly.

No matter what others thought of him, Ranjit lived his life the way he wanted to. He compromised neither on his drinking nor on his sexual appetite. He indulged in them to the fullest but never at the cost of his commitment to the nation that he had founded. He did not permit his driving passion and goal for creating a strong Sikh state to be compromised by anything in his personal life; and therefore, any judgement of him should take this aspect into account.

On the subject of Ranjit Singh's personal life, Fakir Syed Waheeduddin says that 'he was susceptible to feminine influence, but as a man not as a ruler.'

'I love you, Hari,' Suzanne muttered to herself again. Unable to resist the brewing excitement, she sent him another message. 'Baby, dying to meet you.'

She kissed a picture of the old man astride a horse on the cover of the book and quietly slipped under her pink satin bedsheet, fantasising about Hari. He could soon well be the love of her life.

And just before she switched off her bedside lamp, she typed in the words, 'sleeping in lavender' and pressed send.

All her ex-boyfriends knew she was a tease. But what they didn't know was that she was still a virgin... her virginity preserved for His Majesty.

The next morning...

At 9.30 a.m., a long persistent knock on the door woke up Hari.

The early morning hustle and bustle of the tractor and his father's choicest Punjabi abuses at the labourers had no bearing on his sleep whatsoever. The only thing that had momentarily startled him out of his deep slumber, much to his annoyance, was the cacophony created through the village gurdwara's loud-speakers. To Hari's dismay, every morning at the crack of dawn, the temple priest would belt out religious hymns at full amplification. Hari was sure that the priest was playing a CD and not warbling himself. He also suspected that the priest, most of the times, went off to sleep, plugging his own ears with cotton. His suspicions were spot on. Recently, he had heard Mehr Singh, his father's Man Friday, narrate an incident where the village women had beaten the shit out of the priest for playing the loudspeaker at three in the morning.

Conditioned to rise in the early hours to the sound of the loudspeaker and to milk the cows, the women had gone about their daily chores without questioning the time. Strangely, they had found their cows bucking in a manner never experienced before. Finally, when the sun didn't rise in the next half hour, a few of the women walked up to the gurdwara premises to share their concern with the priest. They found him fast asleep. Irritated and angry, a couple of them, Manohar te Balbir di vohti (Manohar and Balbir's wife), took charge of the situation, picked up a broom lying nearby, and gave the priest the thrashing of his life.

'Patandar sabda uluu khich da reha aj tak (making a fool of everyone),' they had told the village elders the next day. Rajinder Singh, the priest, did not dare to look into their eyes, despite being the complainant. Indeed, he had been making a fool of them.

'Hari Kakaji utho, bake up,' shouted Mehr Singh. 'Sardar Sahib bula rahe ne, your phather calling you thale, phor breakfast,' he said in his hoarse voice, parroting the same lines in his broken English a couple of times till Hari responded by saying 'aaya'.

Springing out of his bed, he quickly hurried to the bathroom in search of his pyjamas. If he took another five minutes in reaching downstairs, Mehr Singh would start the knock-and-recite-in-battered-English routine again.

An old faithful, Mehr Singh had been around ever since Hari became cognizant of his surroundings. A few years older to his father, Mehr was Shamsher's estate and farm manager, banker, and security guard. On trips outside the village, Hari had seen Mehr carry a .12 bore gun with him. His flowing beard and twirled moustache added to the majestic looks of his father's 'seculty' man. 'Seculty purpose' was the answer Mehr would give whenever asked about the purpose of carrying a gun. Security was a big thing in modern-day Punjab.

Mehr had been employed when he was in his teens by Sardarni ji, to give Shamsher companionship, as well as to keep track of his deeds. But then, who could dare sneak about Shamsher's activities, as he rapidly took charge of things. Why Mehr alone? For that matter, no Singh of the village could dare utter a word against Hari's father.

Hari slipped into his pyjamas and a kurta and started out for the living room downstairs, where his father would be waiting for him for breakfast, when he realised he'd left his phone in the room. He hurriedly searched for it on his bed and found it tucked under a pillow. 'Two messages' flashed on the screen as Hari scrolled the first one while running down the stairs.

'Bitch,' he muttered as he completed reading the first message. Regretting that he hadn't heard the beep last night, Hari cursed himself. Her voice would have been a welcome addition to the fantasy he had built around her, he thought, flipping through the next message.

'Dying to meet you too,' he typed and pressed the send button. 'Waiting,' said the delivery report; Suzanne's mobile phone was probably switched off as she must be attending college.

However, he was happy to be communicating with a woman so quickly after his first serious girlfriend had kicked him in the butt. He had tried calling her up, but Gaitri had, in bold upper case, texted him to 'FUCK OFF!.' Hari was not to know that the message was instigated by Suzanne.

'Good morning, Dad,' said Hari as he walked into the living room on the ground floor.

'Morning,' replied Shamsher. He was sitting at the breakfast table, browsing through the newspapers while waiting for his son to come down.

Built in the early 1930s, the three-acre Sandhu farmhouse was an array of rooms divided in the centre by a gallery. A veranda ran on the outside along each room, thus making the house summer friendly. The house sat in the centre of the property, surrounded by lush green lawns on three sides, the front portion being tarred for an easy drive up and parking of the vehicles. The rooms had been renovated since the house was first built.

A new wing had been added on the first floor and Hari and Neil had each been allotted a suite to stay in during their farm visits. Ever since Neil's death, his suite had remained locked. No family member had the heart to disturb his things. Mehr Singh would open it occasionally but shut it immediately after getting it cleaned. The family had decided to convert the suite into a prayer room, but that could only happen if Hari's mother mustered enough courage to step inside.

Jaspreet, whose life revolved around her home and her sons,

had been most affected by Neil's death. She had yet to come to terms with the terrible tragedy that had struck their family. She had virtually withdrawn from social engagements and was only concerned with Hari's welfare.

'Slept late?' asked Shamsher, looking at his watch, an indicator for Hari that he should have woken up much earlier.

'Oh yes,' he replied. 'I was reading the book that I bought in Chandigarh. By the way, what does *Sambat* mean?' he continued, making Shamsher put down the newspaper and look up at Hari, intrigued.

'Where did you read it?' asked Shamsher while trying to think of the best way to answer the question.

'On one of the calendars at Bansal's,' said Hari, surprised on noticing his father's interest.

'It refers to the Hindu solar calendar,' said Shamsher. 'Now get ready quickly, as we have to leave for Amritsar to pay a visit to Harmandir Sahib.'

'No, Dad, next time,' said Hari, objecting to the plan as Suzanne's message flashed in his mind. 'I have college and these days they are very particular about attendance,' he said trying to sound very earnest.

'And what are they teaching you these days, may I ask?' said Shamsher hoping to catch Hari off-guard.

'Professor Deshbeer is drawing our attention to an important era in the history of Punjab. We are discussing Maharaja Ranjit Singh,' replied Hari.

'Oh! No wonder I saw those books on your table. Great ruler. But Mehr Singh told me later that you went out to meet Sandy. Is he here these days? Isn't he in Lawrence? Does he have holidays?'

'He developed a chest infection, so the school authorities packed him off for one week. He's fine now and should be back in school soon,' said Hari, his prompt reply to the first question convincing Shamsher that Hari was serious about college.

Raju, the cook, who had just entered the living room with a breakfast tray carrying sausages, different kinds of bread, and mashed potatoes, was asked to promptly call Mehr Singh to cancel their appointment with the senior superintendent of police of Amritsar district, who was to make arrangements for their visit to the sanctum sanctorum through a restricted route. Since the ever-increasing lines of the devotees had become the order of the day at the Durbar Sahib, this kind of access had become a symbol of prestige amongst the Punjabi elite.

As chief of police of one of the most important districts, the SSP, who was accustomed to escorting VIP pilgrims from this route, had offered this privilege to Shamsher. He felt obliged ever since Shamsher had helped him get a lucrative posting in the industrial town of Ludhiana through the then police chief, who happened to be a good friend of Shamsher's.

'Are you sure college is the real reason you want to head back or do you have a date lined up?' asked Shamsher checking with his son once again, before giving final instruction to Mehr.

'Hukum, Sardarji?' asked Mehr who had just walked in on getting Sardar sahib's message.

'Come on, Dad. Why would I lie?' said Hari. 'Mum has also called up a few times to check on our plans. She's concerned about me missing college, so we better rush before we have a situation on our hands.'

And just before he brought the BMW to life, Hari hurriedly sent off two messages.

The first one headed to Suzanne and the second to his close friend Rahul.

'Free in the evening?' reached Suzanne's inbox, who was yet to reply to Hari's previous message; and 'Could I use your house tonight?' beeped on Rahul's mobile who assumed Gaitri and Hari had patched up.

'Dunno. Folks might be home,' responded Rahul, forcing Hari to put on his thinking cap. He had to quickly arrange for a place to make love to Suzanne, if things got hot during dinner. Inside the SUV was always an option, but the constant fear of being caught by the cops was a downer. The other thing he had to ensure was to carry enough condoms. Past experience had taught him to always carry condoms. Pregnancy scare apart, the Romanian girl he had dated for a few weeks last year had objected to him getting too intimate without a condom. And by the time he got one, the libido was nowhere in sight, and they never got into a compromising position again. It had taken six more months for Hari to lose his virginity to Gaitri.

Once out of her class, Suzanne switched on her mobile to find two messages from Hari.

Deciding against responding to the first one, as they always could discuss their relationship once they met, she typed: 'Yeah, I'm free. Pick me up from Sector 34 market at 8.30 p.m. 5683.' The way to sms 'love'.

Eight

'Hari, we ought to do this, honey,' insisted Suzanne as she held his hands in hers while trying to explain what she had planned for him. One of the first few guests to enter Orchid Lounge in the Sector 34 main market, Hari and Suzanne opted to sit in the restaurant rather than the bar. Orchid Lounge had been Suzanne's idea, though Hari had insisted on going to Lava again. After all, last week's night out at Lava Bar had almost gotten him laid.

'Baby, you are taking the matter too seriously,' said Hari as they sat face to face, Suzanne still clutching his hand tightly. 'It's just one of those things and I'm sure it'll go away soon,' he added trying to shrug off the episodes as a temporary phenomenon. 'I just wish it lasts a couple of months, till my exams,' he laughed while thinking about Professor Deshbeer.

'What will you drink?' he asked in the same breath, not giving

Suzanne a chance to respond. 'Let's talk about it over beer.'

'No, you will listen to me right now. If you do as I say, I'll do whatever you want,' said Suzanne, trying to play the role of a mature partner in a relationship that was yet to be established. 'What the heck? Okay. Tell me,' said Hari, a bit irritated over being badgered by her. But then, she was no ordinary woman. Beautiful, sensual, hot, and most sought after! Her floral top with a plunging neckline made her irresistible.

'What do I have to do?' he said, a smile slowly returning to his face.

'Propose to me, you silly fool!' said Suzanne taking advantage of the moment lightening up. And then, she slowly pulled her hands back from his and reclined on her chair expecting him to take over from there.

Hari was not going to let his ego screw up a chance to take a desirable girl to bed. What all hardships one undergoes as a teenager to woo a girl; and here was one ready to be laid if he acceded to a simple request from her. All he had to do was lie down flat on his back on a bed, shut his eyes, and answer a few of her silly questions. Past life regression, he had heard, was all about doing just that. Unwilling to fritter away a god-sent opportunity, Hari got up from his chair in a flash. Going down on his knees, and holding both of Suzanne's hands, he confessed his undying love for her. Unusual circumstances demand unusual responses! And just when he was ready to express his love yet again, the words got stuck in his throat. Uncle Jagraj and Aunty Billi were walking towards him, perhaps to take the table next to them. Not that he cared if anyone saw him dating a girl, because if not now, then when would he do it? But being seen down on his knees was as good as getting caught with his pants down. Even worse! Though from a college girl's point of view, it was certainly one of the most romantic ways of proposing, dogmatic Punjabis took it as a sign of being hen-pecked.

'Hell with it,' he thought, 'Uncle Jagraj was cool and Pussy Aunty (that's what they called her) could be tackled later.' So he went 'please, please' yet again, making Suzanne smile as she looked at him from her chair.

Then she bent down a bit, still seated, cupped his face in her warm hands and said, 'Do you want to kiss me now or in the car, my love?' a response that meant 'yes, I'm your girlfriend from now.'

Allowing her to feel his face for a few seconds, he gently held her hands. Kissing them passionately, he got up and returned to his chair.

Wow, he was in love! It didn't matter at all if Aunty Billi gave a live account of the happenings to his mother via her mobile phone. It actually didn't matter.

Turning up the collar of his bright red Ralph Lauren t-shirt, Hari, who couldn't stop smiling, scrambled for words so as to not appear tongue-tied in front of his new girlfriend.

'So?' he asked.

'So,' replied Suzanne with a grin on her face, fully aware of Hari's present dilemma.

'You sure are a tease!' he said, intending to distract her. He arose from his chair quickly and sealed her lips with his. Why wait to get into the car?

'I am aghast at the public display of affection amongst the new generation. Poor Jaspreet,' said Aunty Billi, tapping Uncle Jagraj's elbow. She was urging him to turn around and see what the lad was up to.

'When we did it thirty years ago, we were considered cool. When someone else's teenage son or daughter does it, it's shameful?' snapped Jagraj, his retort a virtual order to his wife to keep her damn mobile phone back in her bag. What Billi did not see was Jagraj's signal to the waiter, who was standing next to Hari's table, to back off. The waiter was staring at the couple, waiting for them to finish so that he could take their order.

A judge in the Punjab and Haryana High Court, Justice Jagraj's immediate concern was whether this incident would have any bearing when he would pronounce his judgment on a case related to a public show of affection.

Nine

Hari's spacious room located in the right corner on the ground floor of the palatial Sandhu household was virtually a 'no entry zone'. A 'do not disturb' placard hung from the door knob almost permanently or whenever Hari wanted to be left alone.

The illiterate Ram Lobhaya, their house help, also understood this particular English sign and would dare to intrude Hari's privacy only when Hari would upturn the placard.

So well respected was his privacy in his house that Hari didn't really need to ask Rahul for his place. But he didn't want anything to go wrong with the Suzanne rendezvous and was therefore nervous.

Saturday, however, was a new day; and on second thoughts, he really wanted her at home – in his room. Hari hoped Dad would have forgotten the alibi.

He was sure Suzanne would be welcome in his home. The

only blip she might have to face could be a probing glance from either of his parents, just in case Aunty Billi had bitched about their date earlier this week. Suzanne had insisted she come on Saturday evening, a time when LA also woke up as she had been keen to set up the first session under Dr Gilbert Brown's supervision. After all, he himself had volunteered to steer Hari into his past life through a live webcam. But Hari did not want any of it.

'Just you and I,' he had said. However, he had promised to undergo past life therapy on a webcam if Suzanne felt she was not being able to regress him well.

'Nice house,' said Suzanne, as Hari opened the main door for her.

'Thank you,' said Hari as he looked at the beautiful Suzanne with awe. 'Could a girl be more perfect than this?' he thought, and moved forward to give her a welcoming peck.

A perfectly sculpted face, brown eyes, fair smooth skin, well-rounded breasts, and a tight butt – what more could a guy ask for?

'I've been missing you, honey,' said Suzanne, almost apologetic for not being able to see him in the last couple of days.

'How can you not meet immediately after becoming boyfriend and girlfriend?' Hari had argued with her the next day. She had pleaded that her parents had just returned from their pilgrimage and it was not possible for her to leave the house as soon as they arrived.

'Try to understand, dude,' she had implored, after which the couple had fixed a Saturday date.

'Lucky you. God seems to have chosen you as his beneficiary,' said Suzanne as she tossed her handbag on the sofa in Hari's room and simultaneously flung herself on his bed, while taking in the remarkable grandness of the bedroom. Painted a light cream, his room was like a suite. Upholstered in olive green and mustard tapestry, sink-in sofas made a cozy sitting nook about eight feet away from the bed and near the French windows looking out into a private corner of the garden. A sleek study table with books strewn all over was on the right as one entered. A line of almirahs polished in high gloss were on the left.

'What I mean is, first he makes you a maharaja and then he gives you birth in an exceedingly prosperous household. What more can one ask for in life?' said Suzanne as she jumped up again to hug Hari.

She had been missing him so much.

They didn't realise when the hug turned into a passionate kiss. Their first kiss, without the stress of being watched! Cupping her beautiful face in his hands, Hari bit her lips, eating the natural coloured lipstick that added to Suzanne's sensuality. Moaning, her voice a mix of pain and ecstasy, she mumbled 'yes', her words encouraging Hari to move his hand over her body.

'Stop,' she said the moment she felt Hari's hand slide beneath her T-shirt. 'I'm not ready for this yet,' she contradicted herself and pulled back, though her breasts had hardened with Hari's clumsy effort to try and fondle them.

'How much more will you tease me?' asked Hari, who was panting a bit from the brief encounter.

'Remember your promise,' she said, reminding Hari as to why they were meeting.

'Anything for you,' replied Hari.

'I hope I am not pushing you into it, Hari?' asked Suzanne feeling slightly guilty of imposing her will far too much on him. She knew exactly what he must have felt when she had stopped him a bit earlier. But she was sure if she hadn't, she would have succumbed to him.

For some reason, she didn't want to give in on the very first day she visited Hari's house, even though she had been eager to make love to him since the day he had dropped her home from Orchid Lounge.

'No, not at all. But I just hope what you are planning to do isn't too spooky. And I already feel better. The last couple of days have been relaxed. No sound of classical melodies or galloping horses bothering my brain. What shit music Ranjit used to hear!' exclaimed Hari, as he walked towards his music station.

'Fresh lime or coffee?' he asked.

She ignored his offer, as she tried to interpret what Hari had said a moment ago. In one of the books, a past life therapist had outlined how people who experience past life flashes could suddenly go through a quiet period – a lull before the storm – and if their condition was ignored and not handled well, it could quite suddenly lead to very traumatic experiences. Past life therapy was essential for such symptoms as it would help delete images from one's past life that may hinder the present.

'Do you have any music channel that plays Indian classical music?' asked Suzanne.

Her question made Hari grin. Exactly a minute ago, he had trashed Ranjit Singh's liking for classical music.

'Are you sure you know what you are doing?' he asked once again, now cautious and wary. Numerous trips to his village had sufficiently familiarised him with tales of godmen, who cast spells on people to treat them for problems like his. Then there were other godmen who claimed hundred percent successful treatments for pathological diseases. The 'saap baba', it was said, could treat a cobra bite with one blow of air from his mouth. It was a different matter that Mehr Singh's nephew had died due to a snake bite as his family had wasted vital time by taking him to the baba first. Mehr Singh's brother had shot dead the baba in a fit of rage and was now cooling his heels in the district jail.

Having heard many such tales, a nervous Hari was finding it hard to believe that Suzanne was being practical. Why get into past lives when there was so much going on in our present lives, he had argued. 'Exactly,' Suzanne had answered.

In Hari's case, according to Suzanne, digging into his past life was critical to his present and future as well.

'Our past lives determine our present and the future; but in your case they are determining them abnormally,' she had argued in her attempt to convince Hari. 'The obvious cure in such a situation is to take the patient through his past, probing for traumatic experiences which ultimately enable him to come out of the current situation and lead a normal life thereafter.'

'Phew,' he said, wondering what lay ahead. Once again he contemplated on whether or not he should share his present dilemma with his parents.

'Chuck it,' he muttered to himself, finally resolving to go ahead with his girlfriend's request. Moreover, past life therapy was the in thing and it would be cool to preen about it to his friends. In fact, he hadn't caught up with his buddies for two weeks and this would be a great topic to chat about.

'Close your eyes, Hari,' instructed Suzanne. Hari was by now lying flat on his back on the mattress. Soft classical music drifted gently from the Bose speakers that jutted out from the corners of the room. The lights had been switched off, the curtains drawn, and a scented candle gently flickered on the bedside table. The atmosphere created by Suzanne was meditative and just perfect to transfer someone to a state of trance. What she didn't know was whether she would end up applying the conventional psychotherapy method that involved longer and more detailed sessions; or whether things would just come to Hari in a whiff, in which case she just needed to guide his thoughts. She considered herself well-equipped to handle any situation ever since Dr Brown had conducted a few training sessions for her over the past few days.

'Close your eyes, Hari,' pleaded Suzanne. He wouldn't stop winking at her each time she gave him instructions. Finally, blindfolding him gently, Suzanne, who sat next to Hari, once again urged Hari to shut his eyes and start taking deep breaths.

'Take a deep breath. And as you breathe out, sink your lower back into the mattress and feel mother earth taking you in her fold,' said Suzanne, her voice soft. 'And when you exhale, release all your stored-up tension and anxiety. Yes! Inhale and exhale, my love,' she repeated with pauses in between.

Her voice, which seemed distant, was comforting and Hari felt his mind plunge into an unknown world. Suzanne could make out that he was quickly getting into a meditative state and his body was already relaxed – this was a good sign. She could feel his breathing becoming steadier and the muscles lose their initial tension.

Encouraged with these signs in the first session itself, Suzanne asked him to look out for a regal-looking door. 'Can you see a door, Hari?' she asked. 'Don't be sacred. When you see one, just open it and walk straight through,' she said in a soft voice which sounded as if she herself was leading him to the door.

'Yes,' replied Hari, his voice almost a whisper. 'I can see a massive door. It appears to be a regal door.'

'Walk in without fear,' urged Suzanne, though she was tempted to ask if it was the imperial gate of the Lahore Fort.

'Keep walking up the gallery till you reach a staircase.'

'What do you see?' she asked after a brief pause.

'I have opened the door and there is a long hallway. The walls are mounted with exquisite paintings that I cannot recognise. They seem to come from an era that I cannot identify. And yes, I can see the staircase.'

'Take the steps down, Hari. But just before you take the first step, on your left side you will see a table with a remote control lying on it,' said Suzanne, her instructions getting slower and slower with each passing sentence, probably to strike the right balance between Hari's thoughts and her orders.

'Yes, I can see the remote control,' replied Hari, his lips a bit dry and sticking to each other as he spoke.

'Now, carry that remote with you and press the green button when you reach the hall. The moment you press the button, you will see a light flashing in your head and a screen will open up for you. Observe carefully what you see. Those could be images of your past lives. Observe everything minutely. And if you are scared, just press the red button on the remote and everything will return to normal.'

'Yes, I have picked up the remote and I am walking down the steps. Everything is so quiet. No one seems to live here, yet it is so immaculate. Oh! I have reached a hall. Shall I press the green button?' inquired Hari, his tone sleepier than before. In fact, the whisper was so low that Suzanne literally had to position her ears close to Hari's lips to listen to what he was saying.

'Yes,' said Suzanne, by now quite convinced that Hari had actually gone into a state of hypnosis. 'Yes, press it,' she said, repeating her instructions once again, and waited for Hari to be transported to the revelry of his harem.

Ten

*T*en minutes had passed and there was no sound or sign of any movement from Hari. The eerie silence in his huge room was slowly turning minutes into hours and Suzanne started feeling increasingly unsettled with each passing moment. Unable to hold her anxiety anymore, she carefully started observing his abdomen, to check whether Hari was breathing normally. It was okay. This was normal, she thought. His relaxed demeanour was a signal that his mind was yielding to her psychotherapy.

She smiled and decided against disturbing him and waited for things to take their own course.

The next moment, things started taking their own course as Hari's body seemed to stiffen a bit. His face grew pale as if sudden fear had gripped him. His heart was pounding, clearly audible to Suzanne. His right hand was also quivering a bit.

'Please don't set my sister ablaze. Kill me instead,' were

Hari's first words after a gap of several minutes. To Suzanne's utter shock, he repeated the same plea four times in just one minute.

This was not what Suzanne had anticipated. This wasn't what a maharaja would have sounded like or said. On the contrary, others should be pleading for mercy from him.

'Damn it,' she said to herself, trying to come to terms with the sudden turn of events.

Remembering Dr Brown's advice to always remain calm in unexpected situations, she took a deep breath and tried to follow the past life therapist's directions closely. For how long, only time would tell.

Hari's voice changed again.

'I can see a few hundred armed men standing in a narrow lane. I am at the doorway answering the door bell. Most of them are dark-complexioned, and many of them are wearing saffron bandanas. I can't recognise their weapons but they look like indigenous weapons. Yes... a few of them have daggers... sickles, even kukris and some are carrying poles and water-pump handles,' said Hari, his whisper getting fainter and fainter with each word.

'A couple of them are carrying cans. Yeah, cans they are. I can smell...' said Hari, scrunching up his nostrils a bit as if trying to recognise the strong smell. 'Maybe its kerosene or maybe diesel. I cannot recognise any of them. But they seem to recognise us. Sikhs, they say, are who they are looking for.

'"Hume koi haramzada Sikh zinda nahin chahiye (we do not want any Sikh bastard alive), we want to kill every Sikh in the town," they are shouting.

'There is fire with very dark flames billowing from all around.

A young man who looks about thirty-five-ish is begging the crowd... I am trying to overhear. Oh my god... the man looks like my father, pleading to the mob to spare his family. He is still in his uniform. He works as a security guard in a private company and was leaving for his afternoon duty.

'They are dragging him by his collar now and one man is dousing his beard and his kesh (hair) with kerosene. And... they have lynched him. His entire body is in flames... he is running in agony... pain... and a few of the men are now chasing him... he has fallen down on the opposite side of the narrow lane... maybe he is dead... or will be in a moment.

'They are all coming for us. Help! Save us!'

Probably because of not being able to handle the sight anymore, Hari's hand, Suzanne could make out, was trying to search for the remote control. Perhaps he wanted this nightmare to end as soon as possible.

'Please stop them! They have Guddi with them. They are molesting my sister. She is only ten, two years younger to me. Ten odd men are trying to pounce on that girl.

'"Yeh us Sardar ki bachi lagti hai (she seems to be the daughter of that Sikh), iski izzat looton aur kaat dalo (rape her and cut her to pieces)," I hear a young man saying.'

Since Suzanne was not a professional past life therapist, she had in no way anticipated such a situation. She cursed herself for overlooking the fact that Hari could have had many more past lives. She had taken the regression session too lightly, thinking it would be one odd session where Hari would regress to his life as a maharaja after which life would be normal and they would live happily ever after.

'Uncleji is here with the police. He is Papaji's friend and

occasionally comes to ask for votes. He has come to help us. Maybe now we don't need to call the police. My mother is talking to him with folded hands.

'He is not very tall, sports a small goatee, and is wearing a freshly starched white kurta-pyjama. I can hear the conversation. He seems to be telling my mother that Hindus are avenging the killing of Indira Gandhi, the Indian prime minister. She was shot dead by her Sikh bodyguards in the morning and these people are here to take revenge, he is saying, with a grin on his face.

'"But why kill innocents?" my mother is asking. She is on her knees.

'"Behenji, since your husband has been supporting me in the elections, the only concession I can offer you is to not let your girl get killed and raped in front of your eyes. Baki to karna padega..." The operation "Teach Sikhs a lesson" is underway.

'Now they are taking my mother away, dragging her by her hair. This is their concession; to rape and kill her first before they slaughter her children... I can see another group of fifty men coming from the opposite road. They are all similarly armed.

'"Bus yehi ek family reh gayi hai is basti mein. Baaki sab kaat dale (Only this family is left in this colony. The rest have been slaughtered)," says one of them to Uncleji. I can hear him. I am hiding behind our drawing room curtains. They are thirsty for blood! Even a child will do. The only pre-condition being he has to be a Sikh! They need as many corpses they can get to show to their political bosses. They have a tyre in their hand and they have probably seen me trying to peep from behind the curtains. Oh my god, they have spotted me.

'Guddi is still in their clutches. She is now bruised, scratched, and her new pink-coloured skirt is ripped apart. Darji, who lives in Punjab, had sent it for her birthday yesterday. Guddi was wearing this dress and trying to copy Indira Gandhi's action in front of a mirror. "I want to become like Indira Gandhi," she had been saying since yesterday.

'Now I am thinking of ways to protect her. I should get my cricket bat. But I am terrified. I am just a kid of twelve.

'Delhi. Tirlok Puri, is where our house is. Block number 32. It's a small one-room apartment in a cramped alley. I run out crying... helpless, wanting them to take me instead. "Guddi nooh chad deyo. Mainu mar dyo (Leave Guddi, kill me)," I tell the crowd.

'Ignoring my pleas, they tie us together in the front porch and place a tyre around our necks. It hurts and I can hear Guddi crying and shrieking. Her final shriek before she goes to Wahe Guru, where she will ask him what she did to deserve this.

'*Why did you send me to earth if you had to call me back to you within ten years of my birth?*

'They have doused the tyre with diesel and torched it... Mummy, Papaji... Rab ji...'

Suddenly, his voice changed again and that startled Suzanne. Hari was sounding like a television reporter.

'In a matter of hours, Delhi had been engulfed with a dreadful stench of burnt rubber mixed with burnt human flesh. Limbs were scattered on its streets. The orgy of slaughter in Delhi alone, *according to figures*, consumed over 3000 Sikhs, all of whom were either burnt alive or butchered or beaten to death. Women were raped while their terrified families pleaded for mercy, none of which was shown by the goons from the ruling party as they led the mobs. Sikhs were burnt alive by their own countrymen in a state-supported pogrom, the same state that was supposed to nourish and educate us and provide shelter. Our gurus (the ninth guru, Guru Teg Bahadur, was called Hind ki Chadar because of his sacrifice for the Kashmiri Pundits) and freedom fighters such as Bhagat Singh sacrificed their lives for what? So that innocents could be persecuted? So that votes could be gathered in the name of religion? Or is it that under the belly of India's secularism always lay a pervasive hatred for each other, ready to explode like a volcano whenever the time seemed opportune? We need answers. Twenty-four years have passed and only thirteen convictions have been made, and that, too, of the foot soldiers, not the leaders.'

Tears trickled down Suzanne's cheeks, the unabashed cruelty that had been unleashed on Hari becoming unbearable. Clutching his right hand tightly, she lifted it from the floor, brought it to her lips and kissed it passionately, hoping to bring some relief to him.

'Why did they do this to you? Why? Wake up, Hari,' she cried, her tears wetting Hari's hand. 'Press the damn remote. Come into my arms. Why did these bastards do this to you? I am sorry, Hari. I inflicted pain on you. Please forgive me and kiss me,' she pleaded, trying to force Hari to come out of his trance.

Hari, whose state of hypnosis was broken by its perpetrator, was startled to find himself lying on his back, with a girl sitting next to him and sobbing while holding his right hand.

'Why are you crying like a child, Suzanne?' asked Hari, not realising that his past life revelations had traumatised her.

'Why did they do this to you, Hari?' she asked him yet again, unable to comprehend why humans were so barbaric towards each other. 'Is this the price you paid for being a maharaja in one of your previous births – being lynched alive by a mob?'

Hari, who by now had begun to recollect his entire experience vividly, tried consoling Suzanne by saying that the bodyguards who killed Indira Gandhi, trained and deputed to protect her, were Sikhs, and such a thing was not expected of them – killing the one they were supposed to protect. 'You get the drift?' he added, feeling equally traumatised as he became aware of what he had experienced moments ago. Getting up from the mattress, he walked to the mini bar in his room and unscrewed a bottle of mineral water.

'No, Hari, the bodyguards had killed her because they were shaken by the fact that someone could order the desecration of the Golden Temple, the holiest of all shrines for the Sikhs. A misguided step, they were driven emotionally,' she said, her voice still shaky but clearly attempting to explain the situation to him and to herself. 'The year 1984 was a watershed one for Sikhs in two ways. The Sikhs displayed two opposite qualities in a span of five months. Two of the Indian army generals who led Operation Blue Star were Sikhs. Imagine the dilemma they must have gone through while leading the assault. Was that religion or duty? They did not falter and for them the call of duty was paramount as they went about doing their job of flushing out terrorists who had converted the Golden Temple complex into their hideout. Compare them, Hari, to the two Sikhs who assassinated Indira Gandhi. They displayed high emotional character, typical to a race like the Sikhs. Hundreds of innocents were reported to have been killed as the Indian Army's operation coincided with the martyrdom day of Guru Arjan Dev, the person who is said to have fought for freedom. The sarovar, I am told had turned red with blood.

'No, Hari... this is not done,' she said, her tone getting animated, her breath heavy. 'You go about shelling a community's holiest shrine under the alibi of flushing out terrorists, who in any case are there because of your own screwed-up politics, and then expect a community as emotional and fearless as the Sikhs to remain mum? Bullshit! I am a Hindu but my tayaji, my father's older brother, is a Sikh, and I know how he feels about the 1984 carnage, even twenty-four years later. Even, *India Today*, in one of its editions, rated this political blunder as number two amongst the top ten political disgraces in India's modern history.'

'Your tayaji, a Sikh? How come?'

'Yes, tradition. Earlier, the eldest son born in a Hindu family would convert to Sikhism. A Sikh was considered a defender of the country, family, and dharma. My tayaji, Charanjit Singh Sharma, still spews venom at the late Indira Gandhi, accusing her and her bunch of sycophant Sikh leaders of playing with Sikh sentiments in order to woo voters. Just to outdo the Akalis, she and her party colleagues played footsie with the Sikh fanatic leaders, encouraging them to radicalise Sikhs and adopt violent means so that they would be looked down upon as anti-national as a result of which her party would muster all the Hindu votes. The violence that followed put Punjab behind by at least fifty years. When you play such games, you never know the end result. I wonder how Ranjit Singh would have reacted to the desecration of the Golden Temple, since he was such a devout Sikh. He would have marched to the Lal Qila with an army of a hundred thousand Sikh lancers. History says that such was Ranjit Singh's devotion towards his religion that it was under his patronage that the gold and marble work were undertaken on the Harmandir Sahib,' Suzanne explained passionately.

'Calm down. Chuck politics. I'm just a teenager. I have the rest of my life to discuss this nonsense,' said Hari who was now sitting on the edge of his bed, facing Suzanne who was still kneeling beside the mattress.

'Shut up, Hari! Don't talk like a fool. Ranjit was a king when he was all of twenty-one, and heading his misl at eleven,' exclaimed Suzanne, her mood refusing to return to its customary cheerful self. 'It's because our generation doesn't debate critical issues openly that politicians are able to poison our minds with their own vested logic. The media is on its own trip.'

'Hey chill!' said Hari, extending his right hand to Suzanne, a signal for her to come and sit next to him on the bed.

'Ok. Since you asked Ranjit's view, from his perspective, it is far fetched to even assume such a thing would have ever occurred during his rule,' he said, unable to now control the deluge of information welling up within him. 'He was a warrior and not dependent on ballots to establish his supremacy. Furthermore, being a Sikh himself, his kingdom was a de-facto Khalsa kingdom. Let there be no mistake. "Maharaja" was not the title he assumed during his coronation. It was "Sarkar-e-Khalsa". But the present folk seem to have got it all wrong when they claim that this is their attempt to rebuild the lost Khalsa Raj. What they don't realise is that Ranjit Singh's kingdom was established on the tenets of secularism. The decade and a half (1978-95) of violence in Punjab was contradictory to Ranjit's style of politics and governance. If my memory doesn't fail me, Muslims constituted forty-seven percent, Hindus forty-two percent, and only seven percent of the population were Sikhs. Yet the Khalsa Raj was at its zenith during his rule.

'And if one were to draw parallels with the present situation, as by some quirk of fate I have the power to switch back and forth in time, the Akali party, ironically, in spite of getting its Punjab Suba in which Sikhs form fifty to sixty percent of the population, hasn't been able to establish its permanent rule. Why? They have to be floundering big time somewhere, as whenever they have managed to come to power, they have always needed the support of some Hindu radical party.

'Forget the socio-economic aspirations; they could not even meet the religious aspirations of the majority community – the reason why they wanted a truncated Punjab. First they tried to tilt the population percentage by asking for a division of Punjab in a manner where Sikhs were in majority; and when that plan failed to get them a long stint of power, Sikh radical groups, encouraged by the Congress (since the Congress thought it would split the Akali Dal and would also attract the scared Hindu vote), adopted violent methods to get rid of people from other religions and moderate Sikhs. The radicals thought that if they succeeded in getting rid of this chunk of people, Sikhs would be in a position to lay claim for an independent Sikh state, Khalistan. However, what resulted was complete mayhem which scarred the Sikh image.

'And when both the moves failed, the secular fabric proving too strong to be swerved, the politically smart ones, sensing opportunity, quickly shook hands with the Bharatiya Janta Party and won the elections on the plank of secularism. But the sad part is that whichever political party has come to power, it tends to forget its promises and where Punjab's interests lie. They raise critical and vital issues when out of power, but fail to convert their words into deeds when in power.

'Shrewd that he was, Ranjit always kept radicals at bay, who, in spite of having a Sikh rule, wanted a Talibanised version of it,' said Hari. 'Let me assure you, radicals would have found no patronage under his rule as he could differentiate well between lofty misplaced beliefs and genuine grievances. Though Ranjit had raised a battalion of radical Nihangs, he was well aware of their designs. In spite of them forming an integral part of his army in the form of shock troops – as they were one of the fiercest fighters – they hated their king for being tolerant towards the British and the Muslims since the latter had practised innumerable methods of torture on Sikhs. The Nihangs, in fact, were known to have hurled abuses and even thrown musket balls at Ranjit Singh at a parade in an attempt to take his life. However, Ranjit knew that he needed their martial skills and, therefore, bore their behaviour patiently, to the extent of almost getting his butt lashed at the Akal Takht. However, he controlled them with a tight leash by not allowing any of their crimes to go unpunished, the Nihangs would have to part with a nose, ear, or limb depending on the seriousness of their crime; one blow from an axe, followed by some boiling oil to immerse the stump in and stop the flow of blood was all he required for his court of justice.'

Hari stopped suddenly, his outpouring coming to an abrupt halt.

'Shucks!' exclaimed Suzanne, awkward and unwilling to visualise another bloody sight. It had been a long, intense afternoon. Suddenly, she was a young girl again, barely out of her teens, sitting next to the boy of her dreams and eager to shrug off this heaviness, this grave remembrance.

'Yes, I read you were a top-class secularist, Ranjit,' she teased, pulling him towards her as she sealed his lips with hers.

'Hell with the self-imposed regulation,' she thought, allowing his tongue to explore her mouth, driving her to ecstasy. He was caressing her under her right earlobe, something that he had fantasised about doing on their first date at the Taj's Lava Bar. The sweet fragrance of her perfume and her soft moans seduced him as he nibbled and caressed the nape of her neck with the impudence of a consummate lover. Lessons handed out almost one-hundred-and-eighty years ago by a yogi were coming handy.

Still seated on the edge of his king-size bed, Hari slowly moved his arm around her waist, and gently guided her svelte body on the bed, his lips moving down towards her cleavage, eyes not losing sight of the lovely mounds that awaited him.

'Mmm,' she moaned, running her hands through Hari's freshly shampooed hair. Having surrendered fully, she now lay flat on her back, lost in rapture as Hari softly bit her left breast, which had tumbled out from her low cut t-shirt.

She was wearing a black bra, Hari had noticed, his mind now speculating the colour of her panties. Black or red, he thought, as he removed her top....

Temporarily ignoring her right breast, which was still securely cupped in her bra, Hari moved downwards to her belly. Her navel was so tempting that he sunk his tongue in it. Unable to control the flow of pleasure, Hari could feel Suzanne starting to squirm. Perhaps in an attempt to break free.

'Please, Hari, don't stop,' she muttered, her moans getting louder and persistent.

The button on her jeans with 'Levi's' embossed on it was the next roadblock that Hari gently removed and pushed down the blue denims to her ankles. Suzanne obliged him by pushing them further with her toes. She was two thirds undressed, one breast still securely behind the bra and her womanhood hiding behind the thong.

'Ummmmmm…' she moaned, her thighs parting as if urging Hari not to stop.

He hadn't performed this act before, but had watched many porn films where oral sex was shown as an integral part of great sex.

Moreover, the sage's lessons were playing in his head, especially the advice to indulge in as much foreplay as possible.

Sage?

'Don't try mounting her right away. Khelna hai (foreplay)! Play with her. Gustakhi maaf, or she'll joke about you when she meets her friends,' the sage had said while explaining to him the nuances of sex according to ancient traditions. The sage's words were loud and clear, entangling themselves with the images from *Sex on the Water Tank,* the latest porn movie that he had watched.

According to the sage, there were three kinds of women – the doe, the mare, and the elephant. Suzanne definitely fell under the category of the doe, thought Hari, as he reached where Suzanne had been urging him to.

The doe is one who is fair like the champa, her breasts fully rounded and hard. She has a swan-like gait, speech as sweet as a kokila, and a neck like a doe. The mare woman could be slim but can also be fat. She is short tempered, has loose breasts, looks obliquely and walks briskly. She is eager for sexual intercourse and sleeps too much. The third category has disproportionate breasts, a short and thick neck, and fat hips.

'Imagine me as Mohran, your favourite wife,' said Suzanne in soft whispers.

Raising his head and meeting her gaze, Hari reached for her lips yet again. 'Oh Mohran,' he murmured, 'you look so different in the twenty-first century. Can I?' he asked as their bodies wriggled in unison, the burning desire to do it triggered manifold.

'Yes, Hari,' she replied

A cry of pain followed by a fierce bite on Hari's nape signalled a new leaf in Suzanne's life.

'I love you, Hari. I love you, my darling,' she cried, as Hari entered her.

It was pure teenage lust that dominated Hari's room for the next forty-five minutes, the couple's moans occasionally drowned by the classical music in the background.

'I never knew sex was so blissful,' said Suzanne as they lay in bed after a marathon lovemaking session.

'Hmmm,' said Hari assuming her statement to be a compliment to his manliness.

'I better leave,' said Suzanne looking at her watch. It was almost eight. In her heart of hearts, she knew that if she stayed back any longer, discussion on regression would automatically spring up, and that, she wanted to avoid. Hari had already expressed his desire to visit Trilok Puri, the place where his house had been located... in his previous birth.

She was keen to leave Hari fantasising about the good time they had just had rather than the horrible experience he had revealed before sex.

Slipping back into her clothes, Suzanne quickly brushed her hair and put on some lip gloss, hugged Hari passionately, and promising to meet soon, rushed for her car, which had been parked in the driveway.

Chander Bhan, the gardener, who was watering the garden, on seeing another memsahib coming out of the main door, instinctively rushed for his flower pots that lined the driveway. However, on seeing her crank her car with composure, he didn't bother to move the pots.

'Ram Ram! Sab theekan lag raha hai (everything seems to be alright),' he muttered to himself as he saw Suzanne depart in her car at a speed half that of Gaitri's. Her smile was that of a girl fulfilled.

Eleven

The park in Sector 5 on one of the roads perpendicular to Lake Road is undoubtedly Chandigarh's Page 3 football park. Teenagers and young men from affluent families flock to this park in their swanky cars each evening to play a game or two of football. Besides giving them a chance to remain fit in their otherwise sedentary lifestyles, it also provides them with ample opportunities to display their SUVs and expensive motorbikes that can be seen parked along the roads which enclose the park from three sides. Fashion and glamour also get a prominent display, as often amongst the spectators watching the football matches are girlfriends of the rich brats who love to show them off, especially if they are much sought after.

'Hi,' said Hari, waving out to Suzanne from the lake-end side of the park. His team, after scoring a goal, was scrambling back to its defenses, their goalpost being located at the Sector 8 end. He had spotted Suzanne from far, sitting on the railing of the park next to his goalpost. What he could also observe was a palpable excitement building up amongst the guys on seeing a hot girl watching their game.

'Come on, guys!' shouted Karan, captain of the lake-end side team, his voice unusually loud, perhaps an attempt to make himself heard till the other end, where the girl was.

Raghav seemed to have suddenly sprouted springs in his shoes as he dashed to take his back-line position. He had been caught napping a few minutes ago when Daler, on finding the whole defence empty, had single-handedly dribbled the ball to their goalpost, and kicked it inside to take a 1-0 lead in the game. If it wasn't for 'Sekhon Surd' who had just scored an equaliser, Hari's team would have been one down, not a very good position to be in when your girlfriend is around.

'Surd, you see that chick there?' called out Karela. 'She was waving at you. You friggin' know her? Isn't she Suzanne from GCG?' he said, virtually drooling at the prospect of being introduced to a popular chick.

Karela aka Rohan would have got a slap across his face if it hadn't been for last fortnight's incident when Hari had passed a not-so-very-decent remark when Rohan's girlfriend had come to pick him up. Not realising that he was actually dating her, Hari had commented on her sexy legs, making Karela immensely angry.

'Lay off Suzanne,' ordered Hari while signalling Karela to stick to his left forward position. He then dashed towards Suzanne to give her a peck on her lips before the ball came back into play.

'Hi,' she said, raising her hand for a hi-five, an indicator for Hari not to hug her with his sweaty body and clothes.

'Yikes, no hugs right now,' she said. She was dressed in

a nice white polo t-shirt and blue denims that stopped short above her ankles.

'Oh! Sorry,' said Hari striking his sweaty right hand with Suzanne's, giving her a high-five.

'Go, win this game,' said Suzanne, realising how Hari's brief visit to say hello to her had attracted undue attention. Both the teams seemed to be waiting for the lover boy to return so that the game could be resumed.

'Sala lucky hai,' said Karela only to be interrupted by Veer.

'Bull. This chick is not his girlfriend. How can she be? She's friggin' a couple of years older to him,' said Veer, rubbishing the talk as a mere rumour. 'Wasn't she being humped by Kohli phapa?'

'Pass,' shouted Hari, as Karela brought the game into play.

Dribbling like someone who had just been injected with steroids, Hari dashed for the lake-end goalpost, pushing and shoving his way, till the goalkeeper and he came face-to-face. Not in any mood to lose the opportunity, he kicked the ball hard.

A loud crash followed. The ball after passing through the goalpost had crashed into the windscreen of a parked SUV, an Audi Q7.

'My arse is fucked!' screamed Karela from the mid-field. 'That's my dad's new SUV!' he shouted while running towards the vehicle in panic. 'He friggin' paid sixty lakhs for it. You bastard! Didn't you see the damn thing?' he shouted at Hari who was doing some mental maths, estimating the price of the windscreen. 'First you eye my babe and now my car, you mother-fucker!' he shouted, swearing at Hari.

'I'm sorry,' said Hari, walking slowly towards the SUV to inspect the extent of damage. 'But dare you abuse me with incestuous ones,' he said, warning Karela not to cross his limits.

The twenty odd players, a few of them sniggering, rushed towards the vehicle to act as mediators and to evaluate the extent of the damage.

Football was the last thing on their minds. In fact, the entire lot had got a lead story for the weekend – how Karela's dad's SUV had been smashed by a football and how poor Karela had been demoted to a Santro.

Someone had even spotted him riding a bicycle that had a tokri (basket) affixed to the handle-bar.

'Didn't you see that giant of a vehicle there?' asked Suzanne as the couple entered Hari's house that was just a few blocks away from the park.

'I never thought my kick had a 350 horsepower punch. I mean, I just kicked the ball to ensure that it would pass the goalkeeper with adequate speed. How would I know that it would crash land on the damn windscreen of Karela's dad's SUV?'

'Karela? Why do you call him Karela?' asked Suzanne almost bursting into laughter on hearing the nickname. 'He seems to be a cute guy. I wonder what poor Karela must be going through right now!' she chuckled.

A few slaps and abuses would be the obvious fallout of the incident which Karela would disclose weeks later.

'Vadda nawab da puttar (you think that you are some nawab's son),' his father had said, while lashing out at him on seeing the damaged vehicle. 'Chandigarh has spoilt you guys rotten. The village is where you belong. Have you ever heard of a twenty-year-old going out in an SUV worth sixty lakh to play football?' he had shouted while giving Karela a tight slap across his face.

'Phew! I dread to think of that,' said Hari, wondering how

his father would have reacted if a similar fate had struck their BMW. Probably he would have been more reasonable.

'Where are you lost? I'm sure you didn't have SUVs in those days,' Suzanne teased Hari. She didn't want him to slip to his life in Delhi. Ranjit Singh's flashback was more acceptable. He had cried over the phone last night, astonished yet again by his previous life's experiences.

'What do you think would have been my parents' names? Will my grandfather still be alive? You think I'll be able to locate him? Regress me please,' he had pleaded on the phone. 'I am desperate to trace my previous family and meet them. Hug them and tell them I was their son.'

'No, darling. Please don't ask me to do this. I cannot inflict anymore pain on you,' she had said, whispering desolately over the phone. Actually, she herself had been mortified by the experience and was too terrified to repeat the act. 'Hari, I love you. But don't ask me to do this,' she had repeated even though she had this burning desire to probe further into Hari's past life. In fact, she had written to Dr Brown sharing her traumatic experience and asking him how she should deal with the emerging situation. She would probably acede to Hari's request after she heard from Dr Brown.

'Just wondering how my dad would have reacted if I had smashed his sedan,' said Hari hoping no one was home when they entered.

He was also confused about whether he wanted another regression session. It could mean both pain and pleasure. Traumatic experience followed by great sex.

'Hi, Dad,' he said as he saw Shamsher enter the main door. Confused over his father's sudden entry, as just a moment ago he had wished otherwise, he hastily introduced his girlfriend as a close friend.

'Dad, this is Suzanne. My very, very dear friend,' he said, looking first at his father and then turning his head towards Suzanne, who stood just a step behind him.

'Namaste, Uncle,' she said with folded hands.

'Namaste, Bache,' replied Shamsher while the click of the main door was heard. Jaspreet walked in carrying a few bags in her hand. Hari's parents had just returned from the market. They were expecting a few guests in the evening.

'Hi, Mom. This is Suzanne, my friend,' said Hari deciding against emphasising on the *very dear* part this time.

'Namaste,' said Suzanne, folding her hands once again.

'Sat Sri Akal,' replied Jaspreet rather curtly, a hint that Aunty Billi had ultimately bitched. Whether his father knew about it was still a mystery.

'So what do you do?' was Jaspreet's next question, abrupt enough to take away the adorable smile from Suzanne's face.

'She is in GCG,' said Hari, interrupting to reply on her behalf. Before his mother could react, he added, 'Catch you later, Mom.' He said so because he knew his mother could and would go on grilling Suzanne.

'Please send us coffee,' he requested his mother and urged Suzanne to walk in the direction of his room.

He knew sex was out today. And so was regression. His movements would be closely monitored. All thanks to Aunty Billi. Pissed with her tattle, he had half a mind to send her an anonymous note telling her what a nymphomaniac her beloved son had become in the US. He had met Kamal in California and the bugger had turned out to be gay after all. 'Bundu' in Mehr Singh's terms!

According to Mehr Singh, in the absence of girls, many boys in the village were turning gay in order to satisfy their teenage lust. The sex ratio in their village was six hundred girls to one thousand boys. The reason was obvious. The yearning for a male child was not only skewing the state's male-female ratio (873 girls for 1000 boys) but the gender cleansing was turning them into a whopped lot – rape and incidents of unnatural sex was not a rarity anymore.

These low-lives had taken their custom of killing the girl child to foreign shores as well. Hari, during his trip to the US last year, had got interested in the toll free number – 1800-BOY-GIRL! Assuming the dude to be a bisexual pimp because of the manner in which he had advertised his telephone number, Neil and Hari had called up to check if hot Japanese women were available. Hari had been knocked out of his wits to hear the guy at the other end speak Punjabi, asking him the pregnancy details of his wife!

'Which mahina (month)?' the jerk had asked. Hari not understanding what the guy on the other side meant had inquired, 'Japani hai kya (do you have Japanese)?'

'This is clinic of Balwant Singh, Gynaecologist, Caliphornia's most phamous gynae,' the voice had replied, sending the duo into a tizzy. America was indeed queer. You call for a hooker and the guy at the other end asks for your wife's pregnancy details.

'Thank god I have a girlfriend,' Hari muttered to himself, realising how tough it must be to find a girlfriend in Punjab under the given circumstances. Wonder how his country cousins were coping with the girl drought.

'No, Bihra and Bhinda couldn't be gay,' he said, sniggering as he shared his apprehension with Suzanne.

'Chill, Hari. Don't be nasty and I must meet your Mehr Singh.'

'For that, you will have to come with me to the farm,' he said, winking.

'Ha ha! And what about your mother? She seems quite conservative and religious. Is she?' asked Suzanne, realising for the first time that they came from different religious backgrounds.

'What makes you say that?' asked Hari, knowing exactly what Suzanne had meant. 'Oh, the Sat Sri Akal,' he quipped before Suzanne could roll out the example. 'She just returned from the gurdwara and she usually remains excited for the next hour or so,' said Hari, running his hand on Suzanne's face to comfort her. But, deep down, he knew his mother's mindset. She not only had a religious bias, but was one hell of a class-conscious lady too. Whenever she saw a girl with her son, her usual opinion would be that the girl was out to woo her son because of his rich background. Though her hunch might not have been wrong, given Suzanne's attraction for the rich and the famous, Suzanne's relationship with Hari had roots of a different kind.

'Please transport me to Trilok Puri,' said Hari, as he walked towards Suzanne carrying two cups of hot instant coffee. Jaspreet, to ensure that the coffee was to her son's liking, had made it herself, and had the maid take it up to his room. The maid would also report if she suspected anything untoward taking place in the room.

'Only on one condition,' said Suzanne.

'You put too many conditions.'

'No, it's because I need you there. I'll feel secure and protected if you come along. And we can have some fun.'

'Where?'

'Mumbai,' announced Suzanne.

'I've never been to Mumbai. But when and why?'

'November. I am telling you in advance, so that we both can book cheap airline tickets. I can't afford to fly Jet and if we don't get decently priced air tickets, we'll have to take the overnight train, the Rajdhani Express.'

'Why the hell are we going to Mumbai and what do I tell my parents?'

'I don't care what you tell your parents. You have to figure that out if you want to accompany me, honey. I have been invited to audition for a top modelling house. It's been my dream to be a model, and now is my chance. It's one of the other things that I want to try besides becoming a psychologist.'

Hari had no doubt that Suzanne, if given a chance, could set the ramp on fire. She did resemble Lisa Ray, a Canadian-born Indian model who had taken India by storm in the early 2000s. Barring Suzanne's eyes, which were darker, she was a Lisa Ray look-alike. Same chiselled face, frizzy hair, and sylph-like figure.

That had been his first reaction when he had met her on the train. He had wanted to compliment her when they had met the second time at the Taj Lava Bar, but that date had taken another course.

'The only plausible alibi I can think of is faking it as an AIESEC trip.' AIESEC was the International Association for Students in Economics and Management, a highly acclaimed international student organisation of which Hari was a member. Joining this organisation was a fad amongst students as it offered a great platform to meet new people as well as explore the world.

'What else do I tell my folks? That I'm accompanying

Suzanne on a modelling assignment is surely not going to cut any ice with my parents.'

'So then?'

'Then what? Let's go ahead and book our tickets. I think there's enough cash in my bank account for the debit card to be accepted,' he said, breaking into a quick trot as he headed towards his almirah to grab his laptop.

Now she loved Hari more than ever!

Punching the web URL on his keyboard, Hari called out to Suzanne for the exact dates.

Suzanne was amazed at Hari's promptness in agreeing to accompany her to Mumbai without even bothering to take permission from his parents.

'Leaving on 25th November and returning on the 27th,' she replied, without even looking up from the *Penthouse* magazine, which she was now browsing through. She had pulled out a couple of them from the bottom drawer of Hari's desk. Crumpled, they seemed to have been tucked in a hurry into the drawer.

'Rs 16,456 for both of us,' shouted Hari, trying to gain Suzanne's attention.

'Do you plan on posing topless like these women?' he taunted, a little exasperated over the lack of response from Suzanne.

'Mmmm, maybe one day,' she replied casually, without taking her eyes off the magazine.

'Damn it,' he thought. Here he was, doing her a favour by accompanying her to Mumbai. Obviously, the main reason was his possessiveness for her – a feeling that was growing with each passing day. What if she got attracted to someone else? Though he had heard that most of the male models were gay, still... a bisexual dude could steal his girlfriend with smooth talk.

Hari, the sensualist that he was, had other means to distract her from the damned magazine.

Closing the airline website, he opened his music file and clicked on Leonard Cohen.

Suzanne takes you down to her place near the river
You can hear the boats go by
You can spend the night beside her
And you know that she's half crazy

Suzanne, on hearing Cohen, couldn't help but put the magazine down. His song 'Suzanne' was what had stopped her from changing her name to Aarti. Touched by Hari's surprise move, she quickly walked up to his bed and sat next to him, humming the next few lines.

Then she gets you on her wavelength
And she lets the river answer
That you've always been her lover
And you want to travel with her
And you want to travel blind

'Oh, Hari,' she said aloud, thankful to him for playing her favourite song, 'I am so, so looking forward to our Mumbai trip.'

Twelve

'It's a bullock cart I am sitting on. An old man with a freckled face is cropping his oxen hard, urging them to move faster. "Teh teh," he is saying to increase the speed of his cart.

'"We have to reach fast. Nahin to karavaan nickel jayega (Otherwise we will miss the caravan)," he says with a sense of urgency as the oxen break into a canter.

'A young lady in her early thirties is sitting next to me. She is clutching her two children in her arms and is kissing their foreheads. Two boys or one boy and one girl, I am not sure as one child has a long plait. "Ram, Ram," she is muttering, her voice shivering in fear. I don't know her. She just jumped onto the cart with her children. There are at least six other people on the cart, all looking anxious. The atmosphere is one of uncertainty.

'The bullock cart is at crossroads. A sign board on the T is indicating two paths. The left arrow indicates Attari and right, Lahore.

'The old man says "Teh, teh" yet again and steers the cart to the left. He has now brought the cart to a halt and is looking down at the dirt track. They all seem to have gone this side, he says, pointing out to the tracks of the other carts.

'"Thodi hi door mein kafla mill jayega aur sab theek ho jayega (In some time, we will join the group and everything will be okay)," he mutters to himself, but loud enough for me to hear. I am sitting right behind him. I am wearing a white half-sleeve shirt, grey trousers, and a navy blue turban. I am dressed formally to appear for an interview. Hmmm… Yes. Lalaji has called me to Lahore for a possible opening at the General Post Office. Our village is Bassi Mustaffa.

'Lifting his right hand, the old man shields his eyes from the piercing August sun. I get a sense that he is trying to spot the bullock cart train that we are supposed to join.

'The countryside is wet and green because of the monsoon rains. Cannabis is thriving, and wherever land is cultivated, the kharif crop varies from sugarcane, bajra, jowar to a bit of maize and rice.

'It's a semi-metalled link road which Raju Kaka says will connect us to the GT road, leading to Ambarsar. 'Teh teh!" he says and lashes his whip yet again on the animals, urging them to move faster to enable us to reach our destination soon. Amidst a melee of grunts, the two oxen, protesting at such unwarranted beating, break into a canter. The sudden change in gait almost throws us all off balance and we try to hold on to each other.

'Before we left our village, we received a report that said that thousands of Hindus and Sikhs had been butchered by

Musalmaans and they were still slaughtering any non-Muslim that happened to cross their path. Age and sex were of no concern. The opposite was happening in East Punjab, with Sikhs and Hindus massacring Muslims as reports of demarcation of boundaries flowed in. In fact, the rumour was that the Musalmaans of our village, our very neighbours, were contemplating similar action against all of us. The animosity that had been built since 1946 was fast turning into pervasive action in 1947.

'A vulture is hovering over our heads looking down at us, intently. Why? Our bullock cart is not carrying any carcass of a dead buffalo. Now, it seems to be swooping down... but on what?

'"Yeh gidd kya dhoond rahi hai (What is this vulture looking for)?" asks one of the children travelling on the bullock cart, his voice full of inquisitiveness that is propelled by fear. He looks about ten years old and perhaps does not realise he is leaving his village, friends, and school forever. He was given all of ten minutes to salvage whatever he could of his toys.

'A sudden monsoon breeze brings with it a whiff of stench, explaining the vulture's movement. Oh my god! No! Our worst fears have come true. I clutch my scabbard as an instant reaction.

'The "teh teh" of Raju Kaka has become a "puch puch" as he tries to cajole the oxen to come to a halt. The oxen groan yet again, annoyed over the charioteer's indecisiveness.

'Far away in the sky, we can see a flock of vultures descending. They are headed in our direction. And as we follow their flight, we see dead bodies strewn all over. We cannot turn back now. So says Raju Kaka, trying to put up a brave front in this tense moment. His logic is that the Musalmaans have done their job and must have changed their hunting location by now. I agree with him by nodding my head. I instruct another young lad, who has been quiet through the entire journey, to pick up the axe and remain vigilant. "Bhaji, hunn sada ki hoyega (What will happen to us, brother)?" he asks, his voice barely audible because of fear.

"'Ram, tu hi rakha (Almighty, only you can save us)," says the lady, interrupting the conversation. She runs her hand through her children's hair, trying to comfort them. She now pulls the older boy towards her and kisses his forehead.

'A very low "teh teh" by Raju Kaka puts the oxen in action again. But their steps are tentative. Animal instinct! I have heard that certain species of animals can foretell the future. Just as I am about to ask Raju Kaka to consider making an about-turn, we hear loud voices.

"'Allah ho Akbar! Allah ho Akbar! Koi kafir bachke na jaye. Vadh deyo (May no infidel be allowed to survive. Cut them all)!"

'Raju Kaka has miscalculated. The massacre ahead is recent and the vultures were just making way for lunch, the route from west Punjab to east Punjab virtually serving like a food street for them.

'And before we can even comprehend what would have happened to our peers from the neighbouring villages, I see several hands trying to pull out the children from the cart.

'The lady is clutching her children with all her strength.

'But for how long?

'A man, who has an axe in his hand, is now ready to strike her head. He does. Blood spurts from her temple like water from a spring. And before I can pull my sword out from the scabbard, three more men strike her with different weapons, one attacking her breasts, severing them from her chest. Her shrieks fade.

'Now they have pulled out the children and are dragging them to the road. They do not know who to call for help. Their mother's chants of "Ram Ram" were of no help now.

'"Khan, lay ga chuche ki (Khan, do you want to molest the child)?" the man who is holding the children asks one of his companions.

'"Namkeen hai waise (He is quite cute)," he informs him after feeling the butt of the child in the blue shirt. The child is visibly terrified. Unable to take this cruelty anymore, I jump off the cart, swinging my sword in one hand.

'"Teri...Khan!" I bellow, challenging the Khan to a one-to-one fight. "Bole so nihal!" I scream at the top of my voice and attack the Khan, severing his neck with one blow. I can see his torso writhing about violently after being disconnected from the blood supply line and his head lying several feet away. His fez cap is still on. His eyes are closing slowly, as though he were getting lost in paradise, enjoying the dancing movements of the hoors (the celestial nymphs) he might have found on reaching heaven. After all, in his own mind, he has fulfilled his call of duty.

'A swarm of people attack me. "Sardar di gardan vadh deo. Harami kafir (Chop the Sardar's neck. Bastard, infidel)!" shouts one of them. Mohandas Karamchand Gandhi's theory of non-violence had crumpled under its own weight.'

'Get up, you fucking liar!' yelled Suzanne, kicking Hari who was lying on her bed in her bedroom. The present session was being held in the Sharma household since Suzanne's parents were in Amritsar on another pilgrimage, this time to pay obeisance at the Golden Temple. Suzanne's father had just been promoted from a reader to a professor, and his elder daughter had gotten married recently. Suzanne's sister Radhika's wedding, though slated to happen a year later, had to be carried out in haste. Since the US had been hit by recession, Radhika's fiancé's parents were keen for the wedding to take place at the earliest as they feared their son could lose his IT job anytime and then the wedding wouldn't take place at all.

'You are making up this torturous life to make me cry, to screw me emotionally,' she shouted, her voice cracking up. 'It can't happen, it can't possibly happen to someone twice in a row. And why do you remember only the gory and last moments of your life always? No, no way! Get up, you nasty fellow,' she ordered Hari, who was still in a state of deep trance and surprisingly very calm and at peace with himself, unlike the last time.

'Get up! Get up!' she yelped and pinched him hard. He didn't need a remote control to come out of his trance since she felt he was bluffing.

Thirteen

Dear Suzanne,

I just finished reading your account of the experience you had with your boyfriend and I must admit that this type of unusual occurrence is rarely documented.

However, your belief that your boyfriend had cooked up this tragic past life just to torment you may be unfounded. Life is not governed by our logic. It has a mind of its own. My experience in dealing with past life regression cases has taught me not to rule out anything. So please do not dub your boyfriend's experience as fake.

There is nothing that suggests that someone cannot have two or even more violent deaths in his or her past lives. Your doubt arose because you had thought he would regress into his earlier life as a maharaja; secondly, you didn't want to acknowledge that your boyfriend was killed brutally, twice in his past lives.

However, if you are still suspicious, there is a way of validating the experiences by visiting the places and verifying the information.

I would also suggest that if you want him to regress further, please seek professional help. Or you might want to take him to a psychiatrist, if he is showing signs of abnormal behaviour.

You are treading on dangerous territory, which could leave deep emotional scars on both of you, especially him. I reiterate that this could change your lives forever.

Now, go hug your boyfriend. He needs all the love and affection to restore him to normalcy. Life is beautiful.

Regards,
Dr Gilbert Brown

'I am sorry, love. I should have believed every word you had said. Forgive me for the kick on your butt,' said Suzanne apologising for her raucous behaviour.

'How could life be so cruel to you, Hari?' she asked, stretching out her right hand to caress his face.

'As if I have all the answers,' replied Hari who had been quiet ever since they had met for coffee at the Sector 11 coffee shop.

'So you haven't forgiven me, it seems?'

'No, I haven't forgiven the Mahatma. The bespectacled guy with a bald head,' he said looking straight into Suzanne's eyes.

'What about him? He was perhaps the only dude who talked about non-violence in this violent world. He is the father of the nation.'

'Shut your mouth about him being the father of the nation,' said Hari, irritated by her remark.

'Hey! Relax. I know you are going through a rough patch,' she said, holding his hand. She remembered Dr Brown's words – to treat her boyfriend with compassion.

'Who me? I am cool. Dahling... it was you who wanted to...yes... regress me. I was leading a normal life till a couple of months ago, until regression became a pre-condition for sex.'

'But what did Gandhi have to do with the 1947 violence, if that's what you are referring to?' carried on Suzanne, ignoring Hari's outburst, though she felt hurt by his last remark. She was not promiscuous. She had surrendered because she loved him. For her, sex was an emotional experience and not mere lust.

'Come on, now don't defend the guy,' said Hari, loud enough for others at the café to notice the squabbling couple.

'Shhhh, lower... lower your voice,' said Suzanne.

'Gandhi's conceding to India's partition was a cause of boundless violence. *"I am a man of non-violence, therefore, cannot resist the demand for Pakistan,"* Gandhi had said, succumbing to his love for Jawaharlal Nehru. Did he or did he not?

'His initial statement, *"Don't vivisect the country; vivisect me"* – to express his disapproval of Pakistan, soon turned into a whimper. And you still want to call that spineless man non-violent? Just because he offered his other cheek if one was smacked does not absolve him in any way of what ensued. Had your Gandhi sincerely exercised his total moral and political authority, India could have been saved from a massacre, rivalled only by the one suffered by the Jewry of Europe during the Second World War. This one took one million innocent lives that included Muslims,

Sikhs, and Hindus. The violence had assumed the proportions of a civil war.

'Not only did the forced migration lead to all-round mayhem, it also screwed my territory... one that I had consolidated with much pain. I mean, can you dispute the fact that geographically, racially, linguistically, and economically, central Punjab was not *one*? There was no natural dividing line and yet look what they did to Ranjit Singh's empire. You should hear what Professor Deshbeer says since I have been spending innumerable evenings with him trying to understand what actually happened.'

'"They" who? And let me tell you, your professor is passing on perceived history and not history of fact,' said Suzanne.

'"They" means the so-called political leaders.'

'You are being biased here.'

'No. Did I ever condone the actions of my successors after Ranjit's death in 1839. Egged on by the Dogra advisors, they got involved in wars of succession and ruined what he had created. In the end almost everyone lost.' By now, Hari's current avatar was entwined with Ranjit's and his other lives in his conversation and Suzanne had begun to understand the switches.

'Similarly, the twentieth century leadership is responsible for further ruining Punjab that had the potential of becoming the crown jewel of the world and India's pride. The white guys' divide et. imperia (divide and conquer) policy apart, the desis from the Congress and the Muslim League fell into the British trap, who, to attain power used religion as an ace to split the country into two. I mean if you look at it, before this, the communities had never fought for the supremacy of their own faith. History can spring innumerable tales about Jawaharlal Nehru and Vallabhbhai Patel being keen on Partition because, in their hearts, they knew that if it did not happen, power, after independence, could tilt into the hands of Punjab and Punjabis. And since Bengal was also a formidable province, the way they coerced out Netaji Subash Chandra Bose from the Congress is common knowledge. The poor guy had to leave the country and go into self-exile.'

'But history is witness to the fact that Gandhi initially opposed the Two-Nation theory vehemently. The first seeds were sown by none other than the Muslim poet, scholar, and leader – Iqbal. In 1930, he had floated the idea of Muslim majority provinces in north-western India,' interjected Suzanne, unable to bear Hari's, Gandhi bashing. 'You are distorting history. No way am I buying your argument that Gandhi's actions were in any way responsible for the mayhem,' she said sternly. 'He did whatever was in his power to stop Partition. But the circumstances were such that he had to finally relent to India's division. There was hatred all around and Partition was inevitable according to the veteran author Khushwant Singh.'

'Huh!' said Hari, not convinced by Suzanne's argument, as he fulminated about Gandhi in a voice louder than what is suitable for a public place.

The argument, which was attracting a group of students who were also taking a coffee break, was interrupted when the server at the counter called out Hari's name, a standard call to customers when their orders were ready. 'One cappuccino and one Coffee Arabica with milk on the side,' said the server, confirming the order.

'I wonder if this is one hundred percent Arabica coffee as claimed on the poster,' said Suzanne, as she helped Hari place the tray on the table.

'These coffee shops don't seem great anymore. I mean there seems such a difference between the coffee's aroma and its taste. And they are getting more expensive by the day.'

'Next time I'll take you to the Indian Coffee House in Sector 17,' threatened Hari playfully.

'Acha, acha, how many sachets of sugar?' she asked.

'Two.'

'I add only one,' she said, stirring Hari's cappuccino for him.

'You know who suffered the most due to India division?' asked Hari, not willing to give up the discussion.

'Bhaji, Punjab,' said a teenager from the group sitting on the next table.

'You led me to it, honey, and I need to get it out of my system,' said Hari, ignoring the group's desire to become a part of the conversation.

'Don't even for a moment think that my thoughts are disarrayed. So what if I am only nineteen? Remember, Ranjit had become a king when he was all of twenty-one. Man of action, he was. I don't know what will become of my life,' he mused, suddenly pensive.

'Don't worry, dude, we have all suffered the same,' shouted the same guy sitting on the next table. He was desperate to join the conversation for he held almost the same views as Hari's. His grandparents, victims of the 1947 holocaust, squarely blamed the Congress for their plight.

'Professor Deshbeer, who was taken by surprise by my quest for information on Partition, did mention that the idea of Partition had taken formal shape in March 1940 when the Muslim League, at one of its general sessions in Lahore, had asked for greater political autonomy in British India. But I still hold Gandhi responsible for letting it happen. People who lost their families and loved ones, property and homes, describe the polity as something like a condom. They did give the country a sense of security but were actually screwing it.'

'Ha ha!' laughed the folks on the other table, angering Suzanne. Her household literally worshiped the Mahatma. How dare they mock at him.

'Mind your own business,' she shouted, glaring at them. Two of the girls from that gang were definitely her juniors in college, she thought, recognising their faces.

'The Boundary Commission headed by ummm... darn... I am forgetting his name, yeah, Sir Cyril Radcliffe, gave thirteen districts to East Punjab. He granted to Pakistan the richest land – over 150 historical sites... including Guru Nanak Dev-ji's birth place, Nankana Sahib, and my capital city, the beautiful Lahore. The fort on the banks of the river Ravi, beckons me. One of the enigmas of Partition was...'

'He's tipsy on caffeine,' remarked the girl from the other table, the group breaking into a giggle.

'Yeah, my fort,' repeated Hari clenching his fists in anger, as his mind threw up blurred images of the bygone days. 'I mean over sixty percent of the province and more than fifty percent of the population was given to Pakistan. East Punjab, where the majority of the Sikhs presently live, got only two rivers, and upper reaches of the Sutlej, Ravi, and Beas. How does your Gandhi justify this? There is a difference in the Gandhi of history and the Gandhi of faith. Punjab, the land of the five rivers, due to the Congress's policies was reduced to a mere Doab or land of two rivers! Let me tell you, Gandhi was nothing but a by-product of the British policy towards him. Imagine Gandhi's plight if he would have been born in the times of Aurangzeb?'

'He would have burnt him alive,' blurted the boy, now desperate to be a part of the conversation. Hari, unable to take the intrusions anymore, turned around and delivered a punch on the chatterbox's face.

'Dude, you don't know who I am!' said Hari, while leaving the coffee shop with Suzanne following him. Her anger seemed to have vanished and she was chuckling. She was proud to be Ranjit Singh's girlfriend.

Fourteen

*P*icturesque Kasauli in Himachal Pradesh is barely an hour-and-a-half away from Chandigarh by car. Besides being a weekend getaway for Chandigarh's elite, Kasauli's cool climes offer a perfect abode for well-known writers too.

This small cantonment town also attracts another segment – teenagers for whom a drive to Kasauli from Chandigarh is the ultimate expression of freedom. 'Uphill' is the commonly used term. When bikes were in vogue, going uphill with a good-looking girl sitting behind you was the greatest adventure in this town, where social growth had been arrested for a good decade-and-a-half because of terrorism in Punjab. A girl seen going uphill with a guy was considered 'chaloo' and definitely game for a lay. Beer at Dhali, a small village on the highway, was mandatory.

The year 2008 was no different, except that SUVs and other

cars were the favoured mode of transport and the town no longer made much of girls going uphill for a date. The beer shops at Dhali were also out of favour since the uphill revellers could now easily tuck their beers, Bacardi breezers, etc. in ice-boxes. Also the liberal excise policy of the states virtually allowed liquor vends to be opened in mohallas, making the uphill drive a haven for the tipplers. Sadly, some people, owing to over enthusiasm, scripted their own 'downfall' to heaven.

'My dad tells me this was a favourite with his friends for a long time,' said Hari, as the couple passed the small roadside town of Dhali in Hari's Ford Endeavour. 'Chicken or fish pickle was the standard order while all the guys drowned Golden Eagle. He didn't tell me about his girlfriends though, but I'm sure he must have been quite a popular fellow.'

'Your dad's quite a dude, one must admit. And my dad, in comparison, is a total party pooper. A teetotaler, he keeps pointing out the best samosa and gol-gappa places. We had to sneak in Bacardi, vodka, and whatever else we could gather for my sister's sangeet ceremony as he wouldn't allow us to serve alcohol. You Surds na, live life king size, I must admit.'

'Especially me,' chuckled Hari and let out the favourite Punjabi 'burrah'. This was their first date outside of Chandigarh. That both wanted to make the best of it was a foregone conclusion, the only hitch being Hari's mood swings. His past life insights had indeed started bothering him. When they return, she would convince him to meet a psychiatrist to discuss how to meet this challenge. A maharaja in one past life, a victim of riots twice, were too many difficult pasts to live with. The constant flashback was hindering his present life, and Suzanne had already partly started blaming herself for stirring Hari's present state.

But then, Hari's experiences made an interesting case study if she wanted to pursue higher studies in the US. Modelling was never a bankable career, though she was determined to give it her best shot in Mumbai next month.

October is a beautiful time of the year in Kasauli. About twelve kilometres off the Shimla-Kalka highway, the detour from Dharampur suddenly elevates itself into a spiritual treat, the pines giving way to deodars and the sultry heat to cool misty air. The lush patches on mountain terraces offer a natural green bed for couples who want to avoid the now crowded Kasauli town.

A cantonment established by the British in 1842 to beat north India's heat, the town still retains a certain old-world charm, but as is the case with all Indian cities and towns, the burgeoning population and unplanned growth have definitely put its future in jeopardy.

Driving for about seven kilometres from the detour, the couple spotted a nice isolated opening between two mountains and decided to park their SUV right there. The contents of the litter suggested the kind of frequent use the 'concealed meadow' had been subjected to. Used condoms, leaves of anti-pregnancy pills, empty packets of chips, and an odd bottle of beer were all indications that it was a popular spot. Relieved to see the meadow was uninhabited, the couple took out their tuck and quickly made themselves comfortable on a thickly padded spot of grass with beautiful ladybirds scurrying about.

'Ever thought of what you want to do in life, Hari?' asked Suzanne, as she ruffled his hair. Hari was lying on the grass with his head on Suzanne's lap. She was sitting up, not wanting to soil her pink tee.

'I always wanted to be a pilot. Soar high in the skies.'

'So why didn't you?'

'Circumstances.'

'Couldn't have been financial for sure.'

'No. But at present, I feel like joining politics. Actually, maybe an extremist group. The common man is being exploited so much by the politicians of our country that there seems to be no hope. This country will either end up in a civil strife or buckle under its own weight. I have this strong desire to put Punjab on the right track. If not, I might just migrate to America or Canada, like millions of Indians, especially Punjabis, who have abandoned their motherland to pursue dollar dreams,' said Hari. 'You know why I punched that guy at the coffee shop? I was giving vent to my frustration though what he had said was absolutely right. Aurangzeb would have burnt Gandhi alive!' His loud laughter echoed through the mountains.

'So, Gul Bahar, isn't it a bit chilly here? Do you need a shawl? Since Kashmir is ours, allow me the pleasure of draping you in the most exquisite shawl,' said Hari.

'Gul Bahar? Kashmir? What? We are in Kasauli, my dear, and not Kashmir. Though it's my desire to see Kashmir and I hope you'll drive me up there one day.'

'It's a strange and beautiful land of mountains, valleys, rivers, and lakes. Perhaps its beauty has been its undoing, its gorgeous lakes, snow-covered peaks, miles and miles of terraced saffron fields, exquisite crafts, and of course, beautiful women, all proving to be a bane for the land and its people. No ruler worth his salt could think of not having Kashmir as a part of his empire. Never has there been a long spell in its history when peace has prevailed on this beautiful tract of land. Army after army has plundered its vast resources, raped its beautiful women, and killed innocent men and children just because Kashmir was like a trophy on any emperor's map. The Afghans had converted this Garden of Eden into hell, and they continue doing so till date, with majority of the militants being Afghans trained by the Pakistani Army. I think it was, and is, important strategically too. That's what I can infer from the books on Kashmir.'

'I would love to be your begum if you promise the supply of shawls will never cease,' said Suzanne, giving a subtle hint to her boyfriend that he was her man.

'You will have to be one of the many,' replied Hari, who had picked up her hint but was not desirous of making any promises. He was getting what he wanted without those emotional I-will-marry-you kind of promises.

'By the way, maharaja-ji, we are in Kasauli, not in Kashmir ki vaadiyan (Kashmir valley),' said Suzanne, now wondering why was she even bothering to regress Hari into Ranjit Singh's era since he was regressing to that life on his own all the time. In other words, there were no set rules for regression. It could happen anywhere, and anytime, and in any which way. Could he be progressed, she wondered.

'But I read that you guys were very cruel to people in Multan.'

'Where did you read that? Have you been probing into my life?'

'When you were picking up your biography from the Capital Book Depot, I was searching for one too. I saw you from a distance, but was a bit shy to cross your path with your biography in hand.'

'Sneaky!'

'You were always known for your just treatment of vanquished foes, but many historians have criticised the Sikh forces for unleashing cruelty after the capture of the Multan Fort. How do you explain that?'

'Am I being grilled or what? But then, you are right,' he said raising his head from her lap.

'The forces had got so frustrated because it was after seven attempts that they finally laid siege over the fort. The shells of the damn Zam Zama canon kept falling short as we tried pounding the wall of the fort. There was no Bofors and this Zam Zama was supposed to be the best cannon in the world. I had seized it from the Bhangi misl.

'The folks at Multan had dug a wide moat around the fort and had fought valiantly, much to the dislike of the Nihangs. These Nihangs are tough and you don't mess with them. In their heyday, they could kill a man just to humour themselves.'

'How terrible!' exclaimed Suzanne.

'So, the Nihangs placed explosives around the walls of the Multan Fort to create a hole in the wall. But the blast that followed left many Nihangs dead, and boy, were they pissed! In fact, to tame them, Ranjit had to order capital punishment for those found guilty of plundering the homes of the locals. It was an extreme step. You may not know this, but there was no death penalty in my regime otherwise. Except in actual open warfare, I don't remember taking a life. On the contrary, I was very kind to my foes after they had been captured. The ones who died, I married their wives,' he said with a wide grin. 'It was called "chadar chadana". Five or eight, I don't quite remember now.'

'I think there were twelve wives in all, if that's what you want to know. You were one hell of a kinky sardar. By the way, what happened to my Kashmiri shawls, maharaja-ji?' inquired Suzanne, attempting to divert Hari's rant to more pleasant stuff rather than counting his wives, concubines and, mistresses.

'Capturing Kashmir was a great military achievement,' said Hari while sipping a Heineken. He simply refused to stop talking about his conquests, war, or women.

'You are a boastful maharaja.'

'Shut up. It's very vivid... the whole thing. I can actually see General Hari Singh Nalwa leading the charge on his grey Kathiawari horse. His war cry "Sat Sri Akal" is tearing through the valley, sending a chill down the spines of the enemy camp. Hari Singh Nalwa was a ferocious warrior, probably the finest military general in the annals of history because he had the unique distinction of holding up the Afghans and wild warlike tribes. Before we took charge of the valley, the trade routes were unsafe, and all your expensive and precious shawls would be looted en route, especially on the route from Lahore to Petersburg through Kashmir.'

'Ah. I would hate that. My shawls being looted!'

'After Kashmir, we ventured into Peshawar, and Hari Singh Nalwa launched the first attack from Attock in 1818. The ruling tribe, the Barakzai, fled. The residents of the city celebrated their liberation and paid us protection money. But as soon as we left, making one Jad Dad Khan the administrator, Yar Mohammad Barakzai returned with full force to expel him. To cut a long story short, we finally brought Peshawar under the Lahore Durbar only in 1834. Furious over the repeated attempts of the

Afghan rulers to foment unrest, Ranjit dispatched Nalwa to set things right once and for all, which he did ably.

'With an army consisting of 9000 men, Hari Singh Nalwa crossed the Indus and set up an unexpected formation to the west of Peshawar. Such was his reputation that the Barakzai Sirdars (chiefs), fearful of Hari Singh Nalwa, fled the town. In 1835, the Afghans under Dos Mohammad tried to retake Peshawar, but nobody could dare mess with Hari Singh Nalwa. Such was his supremacy in the area that he had gone ahead and initiated the construction of a fort at Jamrud, which formed an important entry point to the Khyber Pass.

'Peeved with this, the Afghans attacked again in 1836, but the Sikhs managed to repulse their fierce attack. Sadly, Nalwa died in the attack,' said Hari, sounding rather disheartened.

'Eureka!' he said, suddenly rising up. 'I think the Yankees need to learn a lesson or two from Hari Singh Nalwa on how to handle the Taliban. If they have even a bit of good sense, they should raise a Sikh battalion pronto and make "Here comes Nalwa" its war cry.'

'What an idea!' beamed Suzanne. Her excitement, however, was cut short by the ringing of Hari's mobile phone.

'Where are you? I want you back home immediately. There is something you need to do for me,' said the gruff voice from the other end. It was Shamsher.

Fifteen

The conveyor belt at the Tower of London, where the crown jewels are exhibited, is an insult for someone who had been a maharaja in one of his previous lives. And for someone who had owned the Koh-i-Noor diamond, to see it displayed in such a manner can be an traumatic experience.

'Sir, how many more times would you be taking this round trip of the crown jewels?' asked the Yeomen Warder who was observing Hari's anxiety.

'Your frequent rounds are causing a security concern, sir. And there is no way you can get a closer look,' said the Warder, a bit sternly.

Dressed in the traditional 'undress' dark blue coloured robe, with red trimmings, the Yeomen Warders are responsible for the smooth flow of visitors. They also safeguard the British crown jewels, of which the Koh-i-Noor remains the most sought after.

Originally said to be an inch and a half in length, and an inch wide, the 105 carat Koh-i-Noor or Mountain of Light, fell into the hands of the British East India Company as a war-time spoil after the Second Anglo-Sikh War. It was set as the front cross of Queen Alexandra's crown in 1902. It can now be seen in the Jewel House, set in the crown of Queen Elizabeth, the queen mother.

'But that doesn't look like the Koh-i-Noor. And, moreover, I had willed it to a Hindu temple – Jagannath in Puri, India. What's it doing here?' murmured Hari, as he took numerous laps on the conveyor belt trying to get a closer look at the diamond. Interestingly, in the year 1526, the Koh-i-Noor had been the property of Emperor Babar, who had valued it at the price of maintaining the whole world for a day.

'Are you sure this is the Koh-i-Noor?' he shot back at the Yeomen Warder, who was taken aback by the lad's retort.

'Another round is all I am going to sanction you to decide if it is indeed the Koh-i-Noor or not, sir, and after that you would be required to leave the premises. Or I shall be forced to call the guards to assist you in finding your way out,' replied the Warder, looking above his spectacles. He meant business.

'I'm not a thief, sir,' replied Hari, deciding not to let his next comment, which was 'how on earth would you know what it took to get this Koh-i-Noor?', escape the confines of his mind. And who would know the real worth of the Koh-i-Noor better than Ranjit Singh himself? The Warder wouldn't have even the remotest idea about the intrigues involved behind possessing the Koh-i-Noor. How it came into British possession, however, was a story every Warder knew by heart.

If Ranjit had to use all the arrows in his quiver to dispossess Shah Shuja, the Afghan ruler and the owner of the Koh-i-Noor, then the British East India Company had left no stone unturned to possess the world's most precious stone from Ranjit's successors. The Koh-i-Noor was made a part of the British crown jewels when British Prime Minister Benjamin Disraeli had proclaimed Queen Victoria empress of India in 1877. Ranjit had no complaints for he knew that anyone in a formidable position would use everything in his power to snatch this precious diamond, and the East India Company was a champion at destroying and acquiring its adversary's wealth.

He remembered vividly the messenger, who, while he was holding court, had come with an offer from the wife of the ex-monarch of Kabul. She was ready to hand over the Koh-i-Noor to the maharaja if he managed to rescue her husband, who had been held captive in the Shergarh fort in Kashmir, and grant him asylum.

This was his moment to strike. To conquer Kashmir, the most beautiful place on earth, and use it to expand into Afghanistan and, of course, possess the celebrated diamond.

'Diwan Mokham Chand-ji, Shah noo theek thak lai aao (bring back Shah with care),' he remembered ordering his trusted general, Mokham Chand, when he was leaving with his troops for Mission Kashmir.

'Heera?' asked Ranjit Singh's emissary the very next day after the Shah had been brought to Lahore safely.

Unwilling to part with the Koh-i-Noor, the Shah had denied possessing it, his answer irking Ranjit immensely.

'Ask him what else does he want in order to part with the damn diamond? A jagir? A few lakhs of rupees or both?'

muttered Hari to himself as he dashed out of the crown jewels hall to take the stairs leading to an adjoining annex, where lay the maharaja's armlet – the one that he used to tie around his arm with the Koh-i-Noor set in it.

As Hari marched up the stairs, he didn't realise that his action of clasping his fists was attracting a lot of attention.

'Anything we could do to help you?' asked an elderly couple, who had come from Chicago to visit London. They were sitting on the stairs enjoying the elusive November sun.

'Koh-i-Noor,' he replied abruptly, the aim of his anger shifting from the Warder to Shah Shuja.

'Seems to be a wee bit upset over the blokes keeping the Koh-i-Noor, I suppose,' whispered the lady to her husband, as the couple, who till now were discussing mutual funds, started debating the merits and demerits of the Imperial government keeping the Koh-i-Noor.

'Arrest all of them and discontinue their rations,' ordered Ranjit, fuming over Shah Shuja and his wife's audacity to breach their promise and not hand over the Koh-i-Noor.

'It's pawned with a money-lender in Kandhar, they say,' said a courtier, who had been sent to get the diamond from the former Afghan king.

'Bakwaas (nonsense)!' shouted Ranjit much to the dread of his courtiers. From his tone, they could tell that he meant business. After all, the battle for Kashmir started with the sarkar's craving for the Koh-i-Noor, and if he didn't get it, they knew that hell would break loose. They shuddered to even think of the consequences. The entire expedition to get Shah Shuja had cost the durbar more than a thousand men and the treasury had been virtually emptied, recalled Hari, as he searched for the section that displayed his armlet.

Shuja, finally on 1 June 1813, after his rations had run out, sent a message to Ranjit that he would honour his wife's word. Hari remembered the march to Mubarak Haveli with a 600-strong cavalry to take over the Koh-i-Noor.

Shuja, after exchanging pleasantries, didn't utter a word about the diamond, his stubbornness to part with the diamond angering Ranjit further.

'Ask him where he has kept the diamond,' whispered Ranjit into one of his courtier's ears.

It was only after Shuja beckoned one of his servants, a eunuch, to get the stone from the zenana that a smile returned to Ranjit's face. The eunuch placed the stone, which was in a small velvet roll, on the carpet at an equal distance between the two chiefs.

After the roll had been unfolded, Ranjit, like a gemologist, had momentarily rotated the diamond and held it close to his right eye to check if it was real. He then handed it over to one of the courtiers, Bhagwan Dass, a hunchbacked fellow, who had seen the diamond before, to make sure it was indeed what they were looking for. Rewrapping it after getting Bhagwan's nod, Ranjit had immediately walked out of the room without even thanking Shuja.

'Excuse me,' said a pretty, blonde girl tapping Hari's shoulder. Hari, who had got a ticket for a boat ride towards Buckingham Palace from the Tower Pier, had been lost in his thoughts ever since he had boarded the boat.

Standing on the top deck, unmindful of the cold breeze, Hari gazed at the Thames, his mind contemplating on whether there was a way of stealing the Koh-i-Noor.

Hari had been sent to England to attend a family friend's wedding as he was the only one in the family with a valid visa. His visit to England and Scotland the previous year had been lacklustre. He had stayed with relatives who had looked after him very well... but in their own way. This time, after Shamsher had summoned him from Kasauli, Hari had come up with one condition – that he be handed enough money to stay on his own. Shamsher had gone a step further and asked him to stay in Central London and see all of Ranjit Singh's memorabilia in the museums in the vicinity. 'Since you are reading about Ranjit Singh, you must visit the museums and see for yourself all that had belonged to the Lion of Punjab,' Shamsher had said, handing him a few extra pounds. Initially, Hari had resisted going to England since he had planned to go to Mumbai with Suzanne. He tried to convince his father, but as it was a close friend's daughter's wedding, Shamsher would have none of it.

'You are a grown up lad... so try shouldering some family responsibility,' Shamsher had said, making it clear that no amount of excuses would help Hari's cause.

'Fine by me, Dad,' Hari had said while offering to pour his dad a second drink as they sat in the family living room, discussing the trip. 'But I have one request.' Looking towards the door to confirm that his mother was not around, Hari shared with his dad the details of his planned trip to Mumbai with Suzanne.

Shamsher, much to Hari's surprise, agreed to his son routing his return flight via Mumbai. The other option was to land in Delhi and head straight for Mumbai with his girlfriend.

The next hurdle for Hari was to find a way to announce his sudden change of plan to Suzanne. She would surely get upset on hearing this bizarre plan, but orders were orders, and staying in Central London wasn't a bad deal either. Also he would be able to take time out from this regression crap. He would convince her that he did not have the slightest intention of ditching her and would surely accompany her to Mumbai. He loved Suzanne.

'Could you click a picture of mine with Father Thames in the background,' said the young blonde, the sparkle in her eyes leaving Hari with no option but to agree.

'Sure,' said Hari, taking the camera from her hands though he was a bit fazed by the words 'Father Thames.' He glanced around for a split second trying to spot a white old man till it struck him that like the Ganges was feminine, the Thames was masculine.

After showing Hari the click button on the camera, the blonde quickly moved to the edge of the upper deck and posed by leaning against the railing.

Moving back a few paces, Hari gazed at her for a few extra seconds through the digital camera's LCD screen. She looked stunning in her long black skirt and a short red coat. The breeze blew her blonde silky hair gently against her face. Her attempts to get those strands in place made her irresistible, thought Hari.

'Cheese,' he said and pressed the button the moment he saw a smile emerge on her face.

'Hi. I'm Hari.'

'Hey, thanks. I'm Suzanne,' smiled the blonde. For a moment. Hari didn't know what had hit him. Why was his life being recycled time and again?

Sixteen

*A*fter regaining his composure, Hari blurted, 'You're beautiful. Which part of the world are you from?'

'I'm from the Midlands. Birmingham, to be precise. Are you from Pakistan?'

'No, no. I am from India. I'm on a heritage trail,' said Hari trying to impress her, but this wasn't too far from the truth. Actually, he hadn't realised that a visit to see the crown jewels could rake up the Ranjit Singh saga so vigorously. During his rule, he had always desired to take a voyage to Britannica with Mohran, his favourite wife, but circumstances in those days didn't permit warrior kings to enjoy such luxuries.

'Never imagined Britannica and its girls would be this beautiful,' Hari remarked, remembering the conversation he had with Captain Osborne on English women.

Suzanne appeared so different from what he had thought

about white women all this while. The oil painting of Queen Victoria in his palace had put him off white women. But since he was always interested in women, he vividly remembered asking Osborne how expensive it would be to maintain English wives.

'I wanted one myself some time ago, and wrote to the government about it, but they did not send me one,' Ranjit had joked with the officer.

'It would be difficult to find one who would be worthy... at least in this country,' Osborne had retorted.

'Not even in England?' Ranjit had probed further.

'Plenty,' Osborne had replied to which Ranjit had remarked 'Ah! I often wish for one.'

Was his wish from two centuries ago about to be fulfilled?

'I am sorry. We in the West tend to stereotype South Asians as Pakistanis and more so since the 7/11 London train bombings.'

'It's okay.'

'By the way, you used the word Britannica? Do they still call United Kingdom "Britannica" in India? Colonial hangover, is it?'

'Huh?' said Hari, not realising why he had used the word.

'And why did you say Britannica is not what you had imagined?' inquired Suzanne.

Hari did not have an answer even though it was only last year that he had visited the UK. Here it was again – the Ranjit Singh effect.

In his interaction with the goras, he had always wondered what Britannica would be like and what made this class of people so different. That he would be drawing comparisons two centuries later was something even his best soothsayers could not have predicted. The treaty of mutual peace and friendship signed at Amritsar in 1809 was one hell of a challenge as he remembered how Fakir Sahib and he had spent sleepless nights trying to read the mind of the Britannica sarkar.

'Metcaffe,' he said, stroking his long salt and pepper beard as he sat on his throne pondering over the future.

'Metcalfe,' said Fakir Azizuddin, his foreign minister (brother of Fakir Nuruddin, the home minister) correcting the maharaja's pronunciation of the English envoy's name. Azizuddin, who was standing next to him in the durbar hall, knew very well that sarkar was edgy at the moment. He was clenching his fists – a sign that he was seriously considering all options including taking the British head-on. Azizuddin, who had never dared to look up at sarkar's face, could see the maharaja's changing expressions through the various glass mosaics that dotted the durbar hall.

'Our intelligence guys told us that since Nepali of France is getting stronger, Britannica sarkar fears that he might collude with the Russians and try to invade Hindustan via Russia, Persia and Afghanistan.'

'Sarkar-e-Khalsa, you mean Napoleon Bonaparte?'

'Yes, yes, the same fellow. The British are keen to stall us at the Sutlej River and turn a blind eye to our expansion in the north-west and north-east because they foresee danger in case France and Russia join hands and decide to enter Hindustan through Afghanistan. They want to sign a treaty that would mark Sutlej as the boundary with us because they see us as a buffer. What if Nepali is no longer a threat? Moreover, there is no evidence of his heading towards India. This would mean they might want to push us further back from the Sutlej. They are already forcing us to make Sutlej the boundary and not Jamuna, as this will give us suzerainty over Malwa and the entire Sikh kingdom. Malwais will die fighting each other if they are not taken under a unified command. It is a custom with the British – first to gain a footing by the excitement of avarice and then gradually assume the governance of the country. Harami... bhenchod!'

'But, Sarkar, if we think for a moment that the French threat is just a ruse, it, however, might prove to be a boon as it gives us an opportunity to proceed towards Kashmir and Afghanistan without fearing for our southern border,' replied Fakir Sahib. He was sure that Ranjit Singh was the Englishman's best bet if they were seriously looking at a buffer state that could line up with them and provide effective resistance against the Afghans or Napoleon. He also knew his king was thinking along the same lines, but Sarkar-e-Khalsa often needed someone to reaffirm and vindicate his thoughts; or he would end up depending on his 'parchi' (slip) system to reach a conclusion. When unable to make up his mind, Ranjit Singh would place two slips of paper between the leaves of the holy book of the Sikh's, the Guru Granth Sahib; the name of the object of Ranjit's wish would be written on one slip, and on the other, the other option or the opposite would be written. A priest would then select one of the papers, and should the one first presented to him prove favourable to the plan of action he wished to take, he would undertake it with great confidence.

Fakir Sahib hoped that if the situation came to a point of taking out a 'parchi', the priest should pick the one reading 'treaty', as he was aware of the fact that Ranjit's forces were not strong enough to fight the British. Ranjit Singh, too, had the same fears and that's why he had once disguised himself and sneaked into a British camp to assess their military might. But his larger-than-life ego could never accept the fact. Though the brave Nihangs were hellbent on taking on the goras and test their martial skills on white skin, the simple spears, inefficient cannons except the Zam Zama, muskets, swords, and quoits were no match to the superior military strength of the British forces.

Fakir Sahib knew that the treaty was crucial for Ranjit, if he desired to expand his rule. And the circumstances were perfect, since both parties would mutually stand to benefit if Ranjit Singh and Charles Metcalfe, the British agent, signed the treaty for mutual peace.

'I am afraid Britannica is nothing but rain and more rain,' chuckled Suzanne pointing towards a flock of clouds that were heading towards their catamaran.

'Let's rush down to the lower level before we get wet,' her voice was urgent. She was familiar with the vagaries of the English weather and didn't want her new friend to get soaked.

'Ha ha!' laughed Hari, now realising why the British used the expression 'it is clearer than the sun' each time they would read out their treaty proposals in his durbar. The other reason he did not doubt Suzanne's description was because it was only yesterday that he had heard the strangest weather report on one of the TV channels – heavy showers will be interrupted by milder ones.

'So are you here to see the Koh-i-Noor?' asked Suzanne, guessing that Hari must have boarded the boat from the Tower Pier.

'Bang on! I'm a research student, researching about a former maharaja of Punjab,' Hari fibbed as they searched for two side-by-side seats.

'Du-leep Singh?' asked Suzanne.

'Who the hell was Duleep Singh?' thought Hari. 'What was it that he was missing?' he wondered.

'I have a friend, Lisa, who has a Sikh boyfriend. He once suggested that all of us drive to Thetford in Norfolk where Maharaja Duleep Singh once lived. I remember him saying that he was the last maharaja of the Punjab, and Queen Victoria was particularly fond of him.'

'And what was Punjab's maharaja doing in the UK?' asked Hari, Suzanne's last sentence suddenly raising his hackles. He was yet to finish reading the books that he had bought. While Hari seemed to possess the power to go back in time and recall events from his previous lives, for some events nearing or post his death, his only source of information, like all normal people, was books or the Internet.

'We've arrived at the Westminster Pier,' announced the guide, whose commentary had become inconsequential ever since Hari and Suzanne had met.

'Wouldn't you like to show me around London?' asked Hari, as they stepped out of the catamaran at the Westminster Pier.

'Beer's on you,' replied Suzanne, her laughing eyes signalling that she was enjoying Hari's company.

'Women are just the same everywhere,' thought Hari. The smirk on his face would have given his thought away had Suzanne been looking at him. He then felt his back pocket to reassure himself that he had enough money for the evening to last.

'You needn't worry about that bit,' Hari congratulated himself on having made the right decision to have shaved in the morning. His clean look was working. Or so he thought.

'So from where do you want to start sightseeing London? By drowning a couple of pints or from Westminster?'

'I'm dying to compare my Lahore fort with the queen's.

Err… I mean, let's see the power house from where all decisions of the Raj were taken.'

Hari's quest had taken him far away from the mission that he had been sent for, to attend the wedding. The sangeet ceremony was to be held the same evening at London's famous Grosvenor House, AJ Marriot Hotel located on Park Lane. He had two options: either to invite Suzanne for the sangeet – that is if she did not have other plans – or to spend the evening with her and call up and apologise to Uncle Karnail, citing ill health. The other thing he had to consider was that the ballpark estimates discussed at his house in Chandigarh had put the per plate price at the Grosvenor at about 250 pounds. Uncle Karnail seemed to have done well after he had landed in the UK in the early 1970s. Real estate was his area of work, Hari's father had told him. Shamsher had even suggested that Hari speak to Karnail and ask him if he could join his business.

'The Palace of Westminster is also known as the House of Parliament,' said Suzanne, as they walked from the pier towards Parliament Street.

'Have you ever been to India?' asked Hari

'Never. But would love to.'

'Be my guest, if you ever decide to,' said Hari, without thinking about the consequences.

'Oh that's swell,' she said, gently caressing his right hand with her left as they walked under one umbrella.

'White women are easy,' thought Hari, but he was in two minds about sex. His desi Suzanne would be devastated, livid, and more if she ever came to know about his exploits in the UK.

But how would she know? He would leave no trace. In any case, he had recently read in a book that people in the South

American continent had sex lives; the British had hot water bottles. He stole a glance at Suzanne's sexy legs once again.

'The majestic building in front of you is Westminster where the two houses – the House of Commons and the House of Lords – hold session,' Suzanne continued sincerely.

Even though Ranjit was weary of British designs, the British themselves had always inspired him. Their clarity of motive, their sense of purpose and the commitment of the people working towards achieving it was something he always cited in his court.

Impressed by their army and its officers, Ranjit had thought it imperative to modernise his army on the lines of the 'Gora forces' if he wanted to defend or expand his territory.

'What a handsome structure,' said Hari. 'Can we take a tour?'

'I am afraid not. The tours are open only till October. They usually start with the summer opening of the house and visitors can actually sit in the galleries to see the MPs and the Lords at work.'

'What next?' asked Hari, looking at his watch. It was nearly one and they had time only to do one more thing before they sat beer-ing or whatever.

'They have my throne... err... the maharaja's throne at the Victoria and Albert Museum,' blurted Hari. 'But how do we reach V&A?'

'London bus, of course. Do you have a day pass?' asked Suzanne.

'Yes.'

Located on Cromwell Road, V&A, one of the largest museums in the world, is spread over seven levels and organised by five major themes – Asia, Europe, Materials & Techniques, and Modern Exhibitions.

'Walk straight up and to your left is the Nehru Gallery where sits Ranjit Singh's throne. Valiant warrior,' said the white old lady as she handed the museum map to Hari. Hari broke into a slow jog and reached the gallery. He stood with trepidation and then stepped inside.

'My god,' said Hari under his breath, unable to hold back his excitement the moment he saw his throne displayed behind a window case.

The Throne-12-Embossed sheet gold on wood and resin. Made for Maharaja Ranjit Singh by Hafiz Muhammad of Multan in 1818 or later, read the citation.

'Come here,' Hari called out to Suzanne, who was gazing at the two huge conical turbans of the Nihangs.

'You see the throne? Those two projecting branches? Each of them was originally fitted with a golden sphere to provide hand-holds for the maharaja when carried shoulder-high in processions.'

'Wow, how imperial!' exclaimed Suzanne.

'Multan,' he said, heaving a sigh. 'Let's head out for beer,' he continued in the same breath.

'We've still got lots to see and the next section displays weapons of Tipoo Sultan,' retorted Suzanne, surprised by Hari's sudden urge to get out. She had been a bit rattled by the manner in which he had suddenly wanted to move from Westminster Palace too, as there was a lot to be seen there. Since he was a research student, maybe he was just keen on looking at things of his particular interest, she reasoned with herself.

'Would you like to be my guest at this family wedding, at the Grosvenor in Central London? Expect lots of dancing and drinks.'

'I don't even know you. How do I trust you?'

'Nobody knows each other when they meet for the first time.'

'But they get to know each other steadily.'

'What's your take on one night stands?' asked Hari, his question nearly making Suzanne jump out of her skin.

'Wow! You move fast,' she said, picking up her glass of Pimms. 'But I'm no pick-up,' she continued after taking a sip.

'I assume you are accompanying me,' Hari said.

'I've promised a friend that I'll be spending the night with her in Clapham.'

'Call her and let her know the change of plan.'

'I should let you know that I am bisexual.'

'How does it matter?' said Hari, handing over his cell phone to her to call her friend. 'You could stay with me. My hotel is close to the wedding venue.'

'You're pulling me in, and the wilder side of me is taking over with each glass.'

'I promise it'll be one heck of an experience.'

Seventeen

'*Bhabhiye ni Bhabhiye,*' the old song blared from the speakers as Hari, accompanied by Suzanne, entered the ballroom where the sangeet ceremony was being held.

Channi Singh of Southall, the father of Punjabi pop, was performing live, and the Punjabis and the goras had just about begun enjoying their scotch, tikkas, and Punjabi beats. Once inside the banquet hall, no one could tell that the sangeet was taking place in the UK and not in a party hall somewhere in Delhi or Punjab.

'Oye puttar, where were you?' shouted Karnail Singh, the moment he spotted Hari. 'Did the limousine reach your hotel to pick you up? I'm missing Shamsher, mera yaar.'

'Sat Sri Akal, Uncle,' Hari greeted him loudly as they did the Punjabi bear hug. 'Aho, Uncle, the limousine was at my hotel dot on time,' he added.

'Please meet Suzanne, a very dear friend of mine. I requested her to come along and be a part of the celebrations.'

'Most belcome, Miss. Most belcome,' said Karnail Singh, who looked rather odd in his stubble beard and turban. He had shaved off his hair and beard within hours of landing in the UK and wore a turban only on family gatherings or religious occasions.

'In Punjabi weddings, all our friends' friends are belcome,' he said, trying to make Suzanne comfortable.

'Please take care of your friend, and Aunty te Nikki noon mila de,' said Karnail waving out to Lord Deadstone, the former mayor of London.

'Great that you decided to grace the sangeet of my daughter,' said Karnail with almost the same fervour as he had shown when he met Hari. Lord Deadstone of the Labour Party was known for his proximity to the Punjabi community as they constituted a significant chunk of votes in south and east London. In fact, in November 2007, Deadstone had made a personal visit to Amritsar to pay obeisance at the Golden Temple after his advisors had said that his visit would get him a majority of the Sikh votes.

'Your uncle seems to be very wealthy,' said Suzanne, impressed by the huge turnout and the very fact that a party heralding the wedding of his daughter was being held in one of the most expensive hotels of London. 'Did he invite all of London or what?'

'How are we bothered? Let's hit the bar; soon it will be bhangra time,' said Hari, seeing a group of dancers already on the floor.

'That guy over there – look, he has a handkerchief in his mouth, a glass of scotch on his head, and he is dancing,' pointed out Suzanne while the couple were heading towards the bar.

'Soon there will be many more like him, including Deadstone. Maybe I'll also join them.'

'No!'

'Cobra, Heineken, or Guinness?'

'Heineken's good.'

'Cheers!'

'Cheers!'

'So is that a traditional dance?'

'I've been seeing it ever since I was a child,' said Hari, laughing as he watched many making a beeline for the floor. The song was Channi's all-time best, *'Sare pind vich puare paaiengee'*.

'So you are off to Birmingham tomorrow?' he asked tapping his feet to the Bhangra beat.

'Yes.'

'May I make a request? Could you introduce me to your friend who had volunteered to take you guys to Thetford?'

Hari wanted to know more about Duleep Singh. How long did his son Kharak Singh's rule last after his death? How did his grandson Nau Nihal, whose wedding he had celebrated with such pomp and show, fare in the scheme of things? The questions tumbled fast through Hari's mind as he lay on his hotel bed.

Suzanne, who was lying next to him with her head on his chest, wondered, yet again, why Hari had suddenly decided to leave the wedding, just when she had started enjoying the Punjabi atmosphere. He was strangely abrupt and she wondered what it was about him that was attracting her. They had nothing in common. Colour, culture, or habits!

'The first and the last time that I'm out with a stranger,' thought Suzanne as she tried telling herself that one-night stands were not meant for her. However, she would fulfill her new-found friend's request before implementing her new resolution. She would plead with her parents to host this Asian guy for a couple of days.

Eighteen

'Buddy, Sat Sri Akal. I am Rocky Singh,' said the tall, burly young man as soon as he got out from his Vauxhall car.

'Hello. I'm Hari.' Hari was standing in the driveway of Suzanne's house in Birmingham.

Rocky was over six-feet three-inches tall, broad, and muscular and was wearing a pair of denims, long and narrow-toed shoes, and a black overcoat. He sported a crew cut, a silver earring in his left ear, and a pencil-line beard that ran along his jaw line. So typical of UK-based second generation NRIs, thought Hari, who had spotted this kind regularly at Jalandhar's Radisson Hotel, and had met similar ones at the wedding here as well. To him, they all seemed like hybrid products because of the similarity in their physical appearance, behaviour, and attitude. Given a choice, Hari would maintain a distance from them.

Rocky was Suzanne's closest friend Lisa's boyfriend. He had

gladly volunteered to drive Hari to Thetford after Suzanne had spoken to him that morning about a Punjabi friend doing some research on Punjab's heritage.

'Thetford is a three-hour drive from Birmingham,' he announced. 'You should have stayed with me, baiji,' said Rocky, embracing Hari, as if he had found a long-lost friend. 'Dad and Mum would have been glad to see apne mulk da banda (person from the homeland).'

'Eh meman only sex lai ne (white women are only for sex),' carried on Rocky. 'You understand what I mean. Hospitality Punjabi, sex angrezi,' he said trying to prevail upon Hari, who had reached Birmingham the previous evening with Suzanne, to shift to her house in Edgbaston, a few kilometres off Birmingham.

'Thanks, mate, for your kind advice and offer. So what makes Thetford so significant in terms of Punjab's heritage?' asked Hari, trying to change the topic as he saw Suzanne and Lisa coming out of Suzanne's house.

'Buddy, you'll learn the details later, but for now, I'm sure you know about the immense dhoka given to the Sikhs! First by the British and then by the Indian government. Dad says Khalistan is a must to re-establish Sikh glory,' said Rocky as he manoeuvred his car out of the driveway.

'But Singh is already king in India. Manmohan Singh, I'm sure you know,' replied Hari, a bit irritated. When will these NRI Sikhs stop meddling in the affairs of the state if they don't intend to come back and live in Punjab? Not only had they deserted the state for greener pastures, but rather than encouraging people back home to work hard and make a living, many, who were totally divorced from Punjab, were always trying to sow the seed of a separate Sikh state in the minds of the Punjab youth.

'Of course. We are all proud of him. But he is not great T-shirt material. He's from the Congress Party na, the party responsible for Operation Blue Star and the 1984 riots. You know what I mean?'

'Friggin' double standards,' thought Hari to himself.

'So if you get your Khalistan, will you and your entire family shift to Khalistan?'

'I'm not sending my boyfriend anywhere. Guys, we happen to be in the car too. And, Rocky, do you mind if Suzanne introduces me to her new friend,' said Lisa from the rear seat.

'A thousand apologies. You know how emotional I get when I meet someone from home,' said Rocky, lifting his right arm from the steering and throwing it back for a kiss from Lisa.

'Hari, this is Lisa. Lisa, this is Hari. My friend from India,' said Suzanne

Turning around, Hari smiled at Lisa and complimented Rocky for having managed to get such a hot girlfriend.

'And I'm sure Rocky hasn't told you his full name. It is Lakh Winder Singh Du-aba,' added Suzanne, fully aware of how embarrassed Rocky felt about his long name.

'Someone's phone is ringing,' said Lisa.

'Must be mine,' said Hari, recognising the ring tone. Digging his hand into the deep pocket of his denims, he pulled out his mobile phone and saw the name 'Dad' flash on the screen.

'Shhhh… Quiet, folks. It's Dad,' he said, before pressing the green button to connect.

'No, Dad. Eh oh Suzanne nahin hai (this one is not *that* Suzanne),' replied Hari in chaste Punjabi, bewildered by Shamsher's outburst.

While Rocky almost burst out laughing, Suzanne, on hearing

her name being mentioned in the conversation, resolved never to befriend an Asian guy ever. Too many hassles in their family set-up, she thought.

'But Karnail clearly mentioned that you were with a Suzanne at the sangeet. Did you fly her in with you? You're crazy. Your mother is livid and she's planning to go to the Sharma household and give them a piece of her mind. You don't overstretch your freedom, lad,' Shamsher said all this in one breath. He was clearly miffed.

'No, Dad. Try to understand. She is a gori. Didn't Karnail Uncle tell you that? He was trying to feel her up while telling her to feel at home at the sangeet. This Suzanne is a friend of mine from AIESEC,' explained Hari. There was so much he could blame on AIESEC. He had done it before and he was doing it again.

'No, I'm not in any AIESEC,' said Suzanne from behind. She hated it when Asian guys lied about their dates to their parents.

'I can hear her voice saying that she's not from that stupid organisation. You think your parents are fools?'

'Will you shut up, Suzanne?' shouted Hari, after placing his hand on the mouthpiece. 'Please don't screw things up.'

'See, she's there with you. I sent you to attend a family wedding and there you are, entertaining your girlfriend,' shouted Shamsher from the other end. 'Phelan Billi saw you in Orchid Lounge doing stuff and now this. You are crossing the line.'

'Dad, I'll call you later,' said Hari and immediately disconnected the call. 'The old man has gone crazy,' he said, shaking his head in disbelief. He had never expected this kind of complication. And that too coming from his dad. Phew!

'I advised you against taking me to the party. You should

have known your folks wouldn't have been pleased,' said Suzanne, irritated over her name cropping up in this manner.

'Damn it. It's not about my family being conservative. It's about your name,' he muttered to himself cursing the desi Suzanne's parents for christening her with a Western name. They could have named her Meena, Ritu, Reena, Dina. On second thoughts, the gori Suzanne's parents could have named her Pamela, Roberta, or Julia... any damn name that wouldn't have created this confusion.

The thought also reminded him that he hadn't spoken to Suzanne for the last couple of days and there were quite a few voice messages waiting for him. Now he began to yearn for her, missing her warm smile, her sexy voice, the warmth of her body, and the way she would cup his face in her hands. The English Suzanne was suddenly getting on his nerves.

Rocky, latching onto the sticky situation, quickly took the first exit for a Tesco gas station that luckily was just a couple of miles ahead.

'Hang on, guys. Hang on. Chill. Any one for coffee?' he said, trying to ease the mood as he looked for a parking slot close to the grocery store. He was familiar with Suzanne's potential to ruin a great drive with her continuous bickering. Not that Lisa was any better, but that was a problem with all the girls he had met. Only degrees varied.

'Get us two lattes,' Lisa ordered Rocky. 'And a couple of sandwiches. We are famished.' One of the advantages of having a Sikh boyfriend was that they never let you pay. And Suzanne, who would not believe Lisa's stories about Sikh generosity, could vouch for that now. The last twenty-four hours spent with Hari in London had been revealing. Perhaps it was a combination of his good looks, chivalry, and his willingness to cough out dough for beer that made it impossible for her to say no to him; and that's why she volunteered to host him at her place for a couple of days as a favour in return. Her parents had protested mildly, but then left it to her. However, what had clinched the deal for Hari was his plea to not have sex when they were together in the hotel room, since he was in a committed relationship.

He couldn't cheat on Suzanne.

'How long do you think it will take us from here, Rocky?' asked Suzanne.

'We've been driving for an hour. Should be there before noon. We took the M6 to Cambridge. We should be in Cambridge, say in twenty minutes, and from there we'll get on to A11, and drive through a beautiful forest. The drive becomes lovelier as we get close to Thetford. Lisa, do you remember the last time we came here? We had got Kittu Uncle, who was visiting from the pind.'

'Gosh, I'm not coming back again and again to see His Highness perched on horseback. This is my third visit, though I pretty much like the Dolphin Pub by the Guildhall.'

'Ha! Don't poke fun at the poor maharaja. Uncle Harinder, the guy who looks after the Sikh heritage stuff in the UK, told me that they had specially designed the statue keeping in mind how the maharaja would have looked with a turban.'

'Didn't he sport a turban? Aren't all Sikhs supposed to wear a turban and a steel bangle, or is everyone becoming like you?' quizzed Suzanne, surprised by Rocky's statement. 'I think it's their striking turbans and impressive beards that make them look so handsome, making them one of the most recognised minorities.'

'Yes. But that's only in the UK and Canada. In the US, they have been shot at, mugged, and assaulted, taken to be Arabs because of their turbans and beards. Remember how after 9/11 many Sikhs were seen wearing T-shirts that said "Don't freak – I'm a Sikh"?

'But coming back to Duleep Singh, the maharaja had become a sahib ever since the British forcibly brought him to England when he was just eight. The child-ruler was made to sign over his kingdom through the Treaty of Lahore in 1846. Duleep Singh was also made to convert to Christianity. In his early days, he is not known to have harboured any ill will towards the British, who put him on an annual pension of over fifty thousand pounds sterling. However, he is reported to have converted to Sikhism after a moderate ceremony in Aden where he was arrested for attempting to visit India after being inspired to regain his lost kingdom. That's why the statue has him looking like a proper Sikh, complete with a turban, because that's what he wanted to be, according to Uncle Harinder.'

'Damn this. I need to know more about Duleep Singh. Suzanne also mentioned his name. Sure you are not confusing him with Ranjit Singh?' asked a bewildered Hari.

'Ranjit was a cool guy. True Lion of Punjab. But what kind of a researcher are you, Hari?' asked Rocky, astonished over Hari's lack of knowledge on Duleep Singh.

'Are you saying this to woo the mem?' he asked in his British-Punjabi accent. Rocky was aware of the lines desis used while wooing blondes. And his friends and he detested the methods these visiting Punjabis adopted. For them, every blonde was a lay. Hari had been plain lucky if he had had a chance to lay Suzanne, thought Rocky.

'I heard the word "mem"... hope you guys aren't bitching about us in *Poonjabi*?' warned Lisa from the back seat.

'Relax,' cajoled Rocky, throwing his hand back once again for a peck. Lisa obliged immediately.

'Was Duleep actually Ranjit's son?' asked Hari, ignoring Rocky's puzzlement at his questions.

'Shhhh! You are not supposed to bring up this topic in the UK. Sardars out here don't like it because they believe he was his son, and the British, as part of a well-planned conspiracy to create misinformation within the Sikh camp, raised this bogey of Duleep being a son of a water carrier.'

'But what if Ranjit Singh were to come in person and clarify this?' thought Hari.

'Ten more minutes, buddy, and the melancholy will stare you in the face.'

Nineteen

The life-size bronze statue of a Sikh rider along the riverside at Thetford was the 'melancholy' that Rocky was talking about. And for Hari, whose mind had been swinging back and forth in time, the gap between history of fact and blurred history of recall was causing tremendous distress.

'*In 1843, Maharaja Duleep Singh succeeded his father to the throne of the sovereign Sikh kingdom of Punjab. He was destined to be its last ruler,*' stated the first paragraph on the plaque below the statue.

'Crazy,' muttered Hari, the moment he read the first few lines. 'My son's name was Kharak Singh,' he thought, aghast at the audacity of the folks, who had dared to change his name.

'Hey, hang on, dude,' he said to himself. Could Duleep Singh be his son who he wasn't able to recall? If yes, which of the queens gave birth to him? Mehtab, no way. Raj Kaur was Kharak Singh's mother. 'Kedi si?' he wondered till he recalled a name. Jindan? Damn. Why was the crucial flashback eluding him, the night Jindan would have conceived?

Duleep, as per the plaque, was born in 1838, just a year before Ranjit had died. He had been keeping unwell for a while.

In fact, flashbacks of Jindan's role in his life had been limited ever since he had started recalling his previous birth. The subconscious mind alternated between Mohran and his Amazon girls, Subhu and Lily. However, the unexpected UK visit had suddenly posed fresh challenges, as life after his death in 1839 stared him in his face.

'Oh Waheguru, don't test me. There is nothing more valuable for a man than his children. What happened to them?' he said, loud enough for his friends to hear and give him puzzled looks.

'Is he fine?' asked Suzanne, looking at Rocky.

'Yeah, just being a bit sentimental, I reckon,' replied Rocky trying to devise a way to ask baiji to move on.

'Jindan, Jindan,' he sighed as one question after the other pounded his mind like the Zam Zama cannon would pound the enemy camp.

'Yes, you were only eleven when I had a crush on you,' he recalled suddenly. Perhaps it was for the first time that circumstances had become conducive for a Jindan flashback.

'I remember your father. He was my kennel keeper. I elevated him to the post of a chamberlain and you were sent to a family in Amritsar to be looked after. You were sixteen when you were presented to me and I couldn't help not taking my eyes away from you. You looked so beautiful in your lovely green salwaar kameez. Soaked in lust, I would visit the zenana frequently. Ah! Those romantic nights in the zenana, they come to me as if it was only yesterday.

'By the way, is the gentleman in front of me, astride a horse, the same fella that you presented to me just a couple of years before I died?' he asked, his eyes suddenly glittering, thinking of the possibility of Duleep being his son after all. He didn't need to clarify anymore.

'Ehna vada ho gaya si (You have become so big),' he muttered. 'But Kharak Singh da ki hoya (What happened to Kharak Singh)?'

Without realising that he had already spent fifteen minutes staring at providence, he quickly pulled out Patwant Singh's book and flipped through the index, searching for Kharak Singh.

Wow! Destiny surely had planned things differently. The information in the book about the events that occurred after Ranjit's death left Hari with mixed feelings.

Kharak Singh had proved to be a weakling and died within a year of Ranjit's death. His grandson Nau Nihal Singh had died the very next day while he was returning from his father's cremation. And the man responsible for his death, they said, was Dhian Singh, the Dogra from Jammu whom he had made his prime minister. Nau Nihal was the grandson, who had been married to Sikh chieftain Sham Singh Attariwala's daughter Nanaki. The wedding had been celebrated with great pomp and show in 1837. The guest list included the rajas of Patiala, Jind, and Nabha; and on the British side, the invitees included Governor General Lord Auckland, the same Metcalfe now Sir Charles Metcalfe, and Sir Henry Fane, commander-in-chief of the British army, who also used his trips to India to gather intelligence that the British forces used during the two Anglo-Sikh wars.

'Rascal! But then no one could be trusted. Take the case of the Dogra brothers Dhian and Gulab Singh, whom he virtually raised from the gutter and gave prominent positions in his durbar. After his death, they took treachery to new heights, which led to the collapse of the Sikh empire in 1849.'

'In 1849, following the closely fought Anglo-Sikh wars, the British annexed the Punjab. Duleep Singh was compelled to resign his sovereign rights and exiled,' read the next lines on the plaque. This troubled Hari further. 'The idiots couldn't hold their kingdom even for a decade,' he murmured to himself.

Rocky, Susan, and Lisa, who were standing close to him, were getting impatient and wondering when the research student would end his work.

'Hey, Hari, let's go to the museum. You'll find a lot more stuff there. No point in staring at the statue,' Rocky called out.

'Oh, sorry, I held you guys up for so long,' replied Hari, quietly putting the book back into his bag. The group then headed for the museum.

'So, any family of Duleep Singh living nearby?' he enquired of the lady sitting at the reception, the moment he entered the museum, which operated from a fifteenth-century timber-framed house donated by Prince Frederick, i.e., Duleep Singh's son.

'I'm sorry to say, none,' replied the woman. 'Certain historians claim that Queen Victoria had actually exerted pressure on Duleep Singh's daughters and Prince Frederick (the only married son of Duleep Singh) not to bear any children just so that the British Raj could tighten its grip in Punjab without the nuisance of potential threats,' she added while handing out a couple of brochures published by a Sikh Heritage NGO.

'Sir, you'll get lots of information from these, but if you want more, there are a couple of books on the front rack,' she said pointing towards a shelf that displayed books on Duleep Singh.

'Duleep Singh had six children from his first marriage and two from his second. And yet, no progeny of theirs exists, which gives a solid amount of credibility to this conspiracy theory,' she added, trying to be as helpful as she could be to the young group.

'Naive explanation,' replied Hari, sounding as if he knew the exact cause of the extinction of Ranjit Singh's bloodline. Didn't anyone research on the fact that Duleep's Singh's father had, in fact, invited this wrath on himself? Legend has it that the tenth Sikh Guru – Guru Gobind Singh – in order to prevent his religion from being pulled back to the 'Brahminical fold', had clearly said that 'whoever erected a shrine in his honour, his progeny shall perish'.

'Sir, if you head for Elveden Hall, which is quite close, you will be able to pay your respects to the last maharaja of Punjab, Duleep Singh. He was laid to rest there,' said the woman, trying to keep the conversation within the scope of her training.

'And once you are done with the books, you might want to walk through the door on your right to take a full tour of the museum. We also have a movie show and only recently have we stumbled upon the gravestone of Rani Jindan. The two-feet by two-feet marble stone that had remained untouched beneath the catacombs of the old Kensal Green Dissenters Chapel in northwest London for almost a century and a half was found accidentally under tonnes of rubble and human remains in the now Grade II listed chapel built in the Greek revival style in 1834.'

'Amazing history,' said Suzanne, nodding her head in awe.

It was a spot where even Rocky had shed tears the first time he had visited Elveden Hall. So, Hari's moist eyes and sniffling caused no curiosity amongst his friends when he broke down while bowing before Duleep Singh's grave that lay in an obscure area of the over fifty-thousand acre Elveden Estate, once owned by Duleep Singh.

'In memory of Duleep Singh G.C.S.I. Maharajah of Lahore. Born in the Punjab, 4th September 1838, died in Paris, 22nd October 1893, Aged 55,' read the epitaph of his son.

All mortals have to die, but whether it was a life well lived is what mattered. Hari had a feeling that Duleep's story must have been tragic. The very fact that this son of a maharaja of Punjab lay in a grave without the dignity of a cremation as required by his religion was a revelation in itself.

Hari needed Suzanne Sharma by his side, for only she could relate to his plight and comfort him.

'Suzanne, I can't wait to be with you,' he said to himself. Though he knew he would see her on Monday evening in Delhi, from where they would fly together to Mumbai, he felt a desperate need to have her by his side at that moment.

The Lion of Punjab felt the urge to share with someone that his youngest son, Duleep Singh, deserved a cremation as per Sikh rites.

Twenty

Going through immigration and customs at the Indira Gandhi International Airport, New Delhi, was easy as the Emirates flight landed at a lean hour of 11 a.m. Unlike many NRIs and Punjabis, who whine about being humiliated by the Indian immigration officials at the airport, Hari's experience with the babu at the immigration counter was uneventful.

Picking up two one-litre bottles of Glenlivet for his dad and a couple of perfumes for his mother from the duty-free shop, Hari walked through the green channel without being hassled. The special gift for Suzanne, which he had picked up from Harrods, was in his Mont Blanc strolley. He would gift it to her in style, on the special evening which he had planned in Mumbai.

Though it had been only ten days since he had flown out of India, stepping into Delhi airport felt weird. As though he were returning after ages, his mind unable to wean itself away from his eventful UK trip. As he lugged his baggage to the domestic airport, which was just a few hundred yards away from the international terminal, his mind wandered between despair and hope. Despair because of the tragic life his progeny had suffered and hope because he had motivated Rocky to speak to his uncle, who ran the heritage trail, to find a way to get the remains of Duleep to Punjab for his last rites.

So lost was he in his world that the banter of scores of taxi and auto drivers hawking their vehicles for a ride failed to break his train of thoughts. 'Bhaji, pre-paid aato. Taxi. Esteem. Quali, Innoba vi hai.'

His mind would find peace only after meeting Suzanne, who would meet him at the domestic airport around noon for their flight to Mumbai. Boarding the morning train from Chandigarh, Suzanne had planned to hire a radio cab from New Delhi railway station and meet Hari at the airport.

Would she be wearing the clothes that he had wanted her to wear, wondered Hari, while anxiously scanning the entrance gate at the airport, waiting for her. He had never realised how just plain lust had turned into love until he went to England. Perhaps it was a trip designed by destiny to make both of them realise how much they loved each other. Suzanne had been missing him equally. And surely, she was wearing what Hari had asked her to. How could she dare disobey a maharaja? Luckily, even though it was November, it wasn't very cold in Delhi and she could wear the same dress that she had worn when they had met at the Taj Lava Bar on their first date.

'Harrrriii!' she screamed in excitement, when she spotted him at the Cafe Coffee Day counter buying a coffee for himself.

He looked quite fresh even after his ten-hour flight. He had shaved and changed into a pair of fresh denims, white shirt, and a camel-coloured blazer during the one hour stop-over at Dubai.

'Suzanne!' he exclaimed, and turned to impose his cup of coffee on a passenger beside him, saying, 'Excuse me, sir, will you hold my coffee while I meet my girlfriend. I'm meeting her after a year.'

He ran to embrace Suzanne, held her tightly around the waist, and drawing her closer, kissed her on her lips, least bothered that public display of affection could get him three months of imprisonment if the cops on duty thought it was an obscene act. What the heck! It was that moment where nothing else mattered.

The kiss was, however, interrupted soon, not by the cops but by the gentleman who had been holding Hari's coffee. 'I need to head to the airline counter, young man,' he said patting Hari's back while Hari's lips were still sealed with Suzanne's.

'Oh, how much I missed you,' said Suzanne. 'And why weren't you taking my calls?' she complained almost in the same breath. 'Met another Suzanne or what?'

Her question, besides rattling Hari for a moment, made him wonder whether his mother had actually stormed into the Sharma household. Hell, no!

'No, baby. Not at all,' replied Hari, confident that his mother hadn't taken any action on those threats. She really was the most merciful judge ever born. If something as dramatic as this would have happened, he would surely have come to know about it.

'Just that I'd left the phone at Uncle Karnail's house and didn't get time to retrieve it till the next function. But I have so much to share with you.'

'Hope you had fun at the wedding?'

'Total fun.'

'Let's check in,' said Suzanne flashing printouts of the e-tickets.

'Is it okay to pile on at your cousin's place?' asked Suzanne while they were waiting for their luggage to arrive on the conveyor belt at the Mumbai airport.

'It's not a problem. He is a pilot with Jet and would be flying on the two days we are staying in his apartment.'

'His wife?'

'He's not married. I thought I had mentioned this before.'

'Oh yes. But I hope no complications? And what about your parents? Do they know about your whereabouts? I don't want to get into a mess.'

'Yes. My dad is aware of my programme, though mom still thinks I'm in the UK and will return on the 27th. That's why I still have my UK mobile phone switched on,' replied Hari, turning his head towards the ocean as their yellow-and-black taxi crawled through Mumbai traffic down Mahim towards the city.

'My tomorrow starts at about four in the evening,' said Suzanne once she had answered her mobile that had been ringing for quite a while. 'Some Imtiaz chap called up to confirm if I was turning up for the auditions tomorrow.'

'Audition? Is it for a film? Hey, what if you get famous? Will you dump me?'

'Hari! Come on! It's an interview kind of a thing where they are selecting fresh faces for top-of-the-line lingerie, shampoos and body care stuff. And I've always wanted to be a model. I had applied for Femina Miss India last year, but couldn't participate since my grandmother had passed away. I am aware of the struggle involved to be at the top, but let me give it a shot at least. We have been asked to report at the lobby of the Taj Mahal Hotel at 4.30 p.m.'

'Hope there's no casting couch scene involved?'

'Hari... will you...' she said once again, this time keeping her head on his shoulder. They were desperate to get out of the traffic and reach their destination, Hari's cousin's flat on Karvey Road, as soon as possible.

Next morning...

'Heck! No! Then?'

'I was almost tempted to steal the Koh-i-Noor till better sense prevailed on me,' said Hari, as he chopped tomatoes in the kitchen to cook scrambled eggs for breakfast, rather brunch to be more precise since it was almost noon. They had slept late.

'You didn't mention all this last night.'

'The music was so loud at the Hard Rock Cafe. The only thing I did was shake my head,' replied Hari.

'And kiss me once in a while.'

'Shut up.'

'But you were also busy checking out that girl in the floral skirt. Weren't you?' asked Suzanne.

'Will you join me if I plan a strike to steal the Kohinoor?'

'You're mad,' said Suzanne who, after switching on the electric kettle to boil water, walked towards Hari to massage his neck and shoulders. He had been complaining about a crick in his neck. He was wearing a sleeveless shirt and she could see where all she had clawed him last night.

Suzanne knew exactly what the Koh-i-Noor meant for Ranjit

Singh. But that the sight of it would leave Hari so anxious had surprised her.

'Did you get the visa forms for Pakistan?' asked Hari, as he threw chopped onions into the frying pan.

'Stop going into your past. And after what you shared with me last night, I definitely think that we should not visit Trilok Puri and try digging into the past. In which case, going to Pakistan to see your fort and the area you once ruled is out of question.'

'I can't forget my past. It haunts me.'

'You must understand... you could be the future of this country. You have the power to see things in the past and the future and take stock of your strengths and weaknesses. Think ahead.'

'Are you trying to lead me to something?'

'Yes. Future-life progression. You are my boyfriend and I will do everything to help you come out of this. I spent these ten days learning progression at the cost of my studies. I love you.'

'I love you too,' said Hari turning around and kissing her. 'I have a table booked for two at the Sea Lounge at the Taj. It's going to be our special evening.'

Twenty-One

A woman is screaming 'Dohai sarkar! Dohai sarkar! (Give an ear to my plea, my lord)!'

This middle-aged woman is trying to catch the attention of the newly elected Punjab chief minister by throwing herself in front of his cavalcade. Her shocking pink salwaar kameez would have definitely attracted the man's attention but for the sullenness in the colour because of hard labour.

She's wearing gold anklets, perhaps remnants of good times, the sound of which is drowned in the roar of the approaching vehicles, which form part of the chief minister's cavalcade.

The cavalcade has slowed down. The middle-aged man from the Congress Party is craning his neck out from the SUV's sun roof. He has just purchased this newly launched technological marvel which can travel on road as well as water.

'Dohai sarkar! Dohai sarkar!' she cries again. Her hands are folded, begging for a minute of his time; he is out on a victory lap in the Bhatinda region of Punjab after winning the 2040 state assembly elections.

'What is dohai?' asks the public school educated chief minister from his principal secretary Birbal Kumar, who has also jutted his neck out to see how the state looks outside his air-conditioned office.

'Gimme a minute, sir,' he says and his head disappears into the vehicle. It resurfaces after a couple of minutes. His face has a happy expression as if he had cracked a difficult Sudoku puzzle. That's how he had spent most of his time during his previous posting as financial commissioner for development – playing Sudoku.

'Sir, I just checked with the head of the History department at the Guru Nanak Dev University. He said that according to a book, during Maharaja Ranjit Singh's time, it was a right the king had bestowed upon his people to stop him by shouting "dohai hove", should they be in duress. But sometimes, people also stopped him just to touch him because they felt he had the power of turning base metal into gold,' informed the principal secretary, mighty pleased with himself for having solved a mega problem in a jiffy.

'And, sir, I have also reprimanded the superintendent of police in charge of the chief minister's security for this breach of security.'

'She seems to have been set up by the opposition to embarrass me. But since the media is around, we must not proceed without listening to her grievances,' replied the chief minister. 'Or, maybe, she just wants to "feel me".'

'Yes, what is your problem?' asked Birender Singh, stretching his neck further to help him hear her better.

The lady, encouraged by the chief minister's gesture, is now lying flat on her stomach and her folded hands are up in the air.

'My husband is on his death bed. Doctors say he has cancer caused by the pesticides in the water. The same pesticides we use to save our crops and provide food for the country have proved to be fatal. We have lost everything ever since the canal dried up and the monsoons stopped. Miles of sand, which you see on your right, was once farmland. And we owned fifty acres of land,' she claims. She is urging the chief minister to look up at the sand dunes and cacti, and imagine her plight.

'Please save us from this economic penury. We used to produce the finest paddy and now we don't have a morsel to eat. The farm equipment has no buyer and we still owe money to the bank. No one is willing to buy it as there is no more agriculture taking place. Dohai, sarkar, dohai,' she pleads.

'Sir, I have spoken to the local deputy commissioner and asked him to look into this particular case,' whispered the principal secretary in the chief minister's ears.

'Bibi... DC noon mil le. Keh ditta hai (meet the DC. He has been informed),' says the chief minister.

'Sir, had these officers been capable of solving our problems why would we have come begging to you?' she wails helplessly.

Her wails, however, fade into oblivion; the SUV's roar making a deafening sound as the driver presses the accelerator to proceed. An industrialist was waiting for the chief minister at the Public Works Department guest house with a proposal for a Special Futuristic Zone. Since South Punjab had virtually become a desert, there was a great opportunity for converting it into the gambling capital of India, along the lines of Las Vegas and Macau in the USA and China, respectively.

A secret survey had revealed that many girls belonging to families that were once rich because of the Green Revolution, were now willing to work as bar dancers, waitresses, and stewards. Former farmers had also shown eagerness to be employed as guards, chauffeurs, and waiters.

This meeting with the newly elected chief minister was crucial for Ribhu Bhai Goel because the Central Government had planned a major rehabilitation program (Punjab Bachao Yojna) by offering great incentives and subsidies on micro-sprinkler and drip-irrigation techniques. For Plan 'Las Vegas' to unfold, the proposal had to be held back. The previous incumbent from the Congress had not allowed its implementation and it was important that the new incumbent did the same. Cost was of no concern for Ribhu Bhai.

'My Punjab. Every turn is a blind alley,' muttered Hari, sounding helpless at the sight of things to come.

Suzanne had finally prevailed upon Hari to allow her to progress him into his future life. Though that was not her main motive, as she had sincerely wanted to help him, Suzanne had hoped that if Hari progressed into the future, he might just mention where their affair had headed.

'There is this tall young man. He seems to be in his early thirties. His eyes are bright blue, his beard slightly blonde. He is wearing a cream-coloured turban, a khaki shirt, and blue denims. He is sitting under a candle-lit lamp in a small room...

seems like a study as it has books. Who is he... and why is he so significant?

'He is browsing through a report and making notes. It's an old 2009 report by Mathew Rodell of NASA, warning that if suitable measures were not taken, North India could soon become a desert. He is bracing himself for a long crusade to set things in order.

'He also has in his possession, information sought under the Right to Information Act about the Punjab Bachao Yojna under which the Central Government had earmarked Rs 100,000 crores to rejuvenate Punjab's ground water, agriculture, and businesses, but strangely none of it was utilised.

'He will fight to the last drop of his blood to restore Punjab's lost glory. To put it back in its rightful place as India's number one state. He has vowed to free it from the greedy and power-hungry politicians, who in spite of getting all kind of resources and facilities to make Punjab prosperous, have chosen to fill their own coffer, even if that meant promoting anarchy, poverty, and environmental degradation.'

Suddenly his voice changed. 'Oh shucks! Michael Jackson will die next year, India's home minister will get a shoe hurled at him by a Sikh journalist, who is asking him questions about bringing to justice the perpetrators of the 1984 Sikh riots. Manmohan Singh will be back as the Indian prime minister and he will head a very corrupt government in his second term.'

'How the hell will Michael Jackson die?' asked Suzanne, interrupting his flow of thoughts. 'I love his music. It'll be a great loss to music lovers. America's journey from Jackson to Obama has been rapid. I mean if there had been no Jackson, an Obama might also not have been possible. Jackson's music, at some level, helped change the mindset of the white community.'

—◦◦◎◦

'Birbal, what is that ramshackle structure over there I see?'
Birender Singh asks his principal secretary. He is pointing his
finger towards a dilapidated two-storey building.

'Seems like an abandoned government school, sir, given the
wild growth of cannabis in the yard and roots of banyan trees
jutting out of the rooms.'

'Why abandoned? No children study here?'

'Gimme a minute, sir,' says Birbal. He orders his peon to
call the watchman if there was one and probe the matter.

'Time pass hai, sarkar. You will find all the children near the
police station,' said Balkar Singh, the school chowkidar.

'Police station?'

'Yes, sir. Cheap drugs are available. The local SHO is the
MLA's own guy and he trades drugs through the police station.
Safest place. All children are addicted to drugs and it has been
a couple of years since any child came to the school. The
government teachers now teach in private schools and they
draw their salaries from both the places. Bus time pass hai,
sarkar... kade koi aauga soorma te shayad asi vi sir chak ke
kavange, eh dekho mera desh Punjab. Gustakhi maaf jannab
(some super hero will be born one day who will turn Punjab
into a prosperous land and we will be able to once again call
ourselves Punjabis with pride),' he said while bowing his head
to the chief minister.

—◦◦◎◦

By now, Hari had been completely transported into the future. Though there were disturbing images that were being transmitted, unlike previously, he was not rattled by them.

The victory lap has made its way into the Doaba districts comprising Kapurthala, Hoshiarpur, Garhshankar, Jalandhar, Nakodar, Banga, and Nawanshahr. The victory lap is akin to the Ashvamedha Yajna, where kings in ancient times, to mark their sovereignty and power, used to let loose a stallion and dared anybody to challenge their supremacy.

The modern version of the Ashwamedha is the 'Dhakka Yajna' (display of bullying power). It is conducted usually on an SUV, where the state forcibly pulls out people and children from their homes and schools respectively and lines them along the route through which the newly elected chief minister has to pass.

One such human chain is on the Hoshiarpur-Jalandhar road, starting from Adampur and goes towards Jalandhar.

'Where are the men?' muttered Hari

'I only see women and children. Where are the men folk, Birbal?' asks Birender looking down from the SUV's sun roof towards his principal secretary, who is crouched inside the vehicle.

'Gimme a minute, sir,' replies Birbal. After making a few phone calls, he gets up and reaches for the chief minister's left ear.

'Sir, the district police chief says all the available men have been pulled out. Others have left their homes for western countries. You see the previous governments have been unable to provide worthwhile job opportunities for the youth resulting in mass exodus of young Punjabi men to western and middle-eastern countries from the mid-twentieth century onwards. So desperate were they for a better livelihood that many even risked their lives by taking treacherous routes, also called "donkey lagana" (backpacking through snow) to enter their country of choice. In the year 1990, over three hundred Punjabis had died in the Mediterranean Sea while they were being transported in a vessel to be smuggled into Italy.'

'But then what happens to these women?'

'Nothing, sir. They have been languishing here for years, tortured by their in-laws. The problem of runaway bridegrooms has been prevalent since decades with the state unable to append new laws to save them. And the children, you see, they have been raised without their fathers being at home. It is good that the police pulled out the folks from their homes, otherwise we would have been oblivious to the problem,' said Birbal.

'Well done, Birbal. It is not without reason that I chose you as my principal secretary.'

'Thank you, sir. May I request you to consider appointing Balwant Singh as your additional principal secretary? He is equally resourceful. And Ram Inder Singh Sidhu would be a perfect choice for the post of director general of police. He is affable and yielding. A tyrant for the masses and a lamb in front of political authority.'

'But isn't this true of the entire Punjab police?'

'Sir,' said Birbal, realising he might have over stepped his jurisdiction. But then he was testing waters.

'I see the same young lad again scribbling something frantically,' said Hari, this time getting a bit restless.

'What else do you see?' asked Suzanne, urging Hari to look

for clues. 'What is he wearing? See if there is a name plate around. You might get a hint.'

'I don't believe this. I love you, Suzanne,' shrieked Hari, suddenly getting up from his trance with a sense or urgency. Hugging Suzzane warmly, he said, 'We have been blessed to be together forever.'

Twenty-Two

The wide smile on Suzanne's face was for two special reasons. Her modelling mission had been quite successful with lingerie giant Victoria's Secret asking her to appear for an audition for their upcoming range of bikinis. Secondly, Hari's comment, even though he had abruptly got up from his progression, had re-reassured her that their relationship would ultimately culminate in marriage.

The Sea Lounge at the Taj Mahal Hotel, overlooking the Gateway of India and the harbour on the Arabian Sea, was the perfect place to celebrate these two eventualities. Her boyfriend probably guessed her mood and booked a table at the right spot, next to the gigantic windows overlooking the harbour. What she didn't realise was that he had made this reservation when he was in England. He had wanted to gift his girlfriend in style the special thing he had bought for her from England.

Showing no anxiety at all, Hari pulled out a small jewellery case from his pocket and asked Suzanne to open her eyes, which she had shut a second ago on Hari's orders.

'What is it, Hari?' she asked, seeing the box which had the word 'Harrods' inscribed on it.

'Open it,' said Hari in an adoring tone.

'Oh my god! It's an eternity ring. Propose to me and put it on my finger.'

'I cannot live without you,' said Hari as a tear trickled down his cheek. 'I realised in England, how helpless I was without you,' his voice nearly choking with emotion, leaving Suzanne quite surprised.

What was wrong with him?

Cupping his face with both her hands, she murmured, 'This is the happiest moment for both of us. We must celebrate.'

The ensuing gun-shots were similar to an ode, as back home, his friends would have celebrated this moment by firing in the air with their expensive Berettas.

Chandigarh
Three days later: 29 November

The sea of mourners assembled at Chandigarh's Sector 25 cremation ground indicated that a person of the stature of a maharaja must have died. And anyone who would have seen Hari's jewelled regalia while undertaking his last journey in this lifetime would have been easily convinced that the lad indeed had royal blood.

The three-day siege of the Taj Mahal Hotel in Colaba, Mumbai, starting on the 26th, by Pakistan-based terrorists belonging to the Lashkar-e-Taiba had left many dead.

Hari had also been hit by bullets while saving his girlfriend, murmured mourners, anxious to have a look at Suzanne, who was believed to have guarded Hari's dead body for two days, lest it be destroyed in the fire that had engulfed the Sea Lounge after terrorists had held siege for over sixty hours.

Initial reports indicated that ten terrorists had entered Mumbai through the Arabian Sea and led at least ten coordinated bomb and gun attacks on India's financial capital, the attack on the Taj Mahal Hotel being the most ghastly.

Hari needed a cremation befitting a hero as well as a maharaja, a maharaja who was killed incongruously by men who would have been hitherto his subjects from his kingdom's capital, Lahore.

No amount of pressure from her family or the psychiatrist could keep Suzanne away from attending the maharaja's last journey.

Three days of bloodshed, bullet shots, grenade explosions, fire, and death all around had wrecked her and she blamed herself for this grave tragedy in her life.

Why did I force Hari to come to Mumbai? Why did I give him pain and agony by regressing him? Was Hari aware of the events that would follow after he had been progressed? If he was, why didn't he prevent his death by not going to the Taj? What did he mean when he said, 'I can't live without you?' were the questions that pounded Suzanne's fragile mind as she saw Shamsher Uncle light his nineteen-year-old son's pyre. Writ on his face besides tremendous grief, she thought, was a chargesheet against her.

30 November, newspaper headlines

Chandigarh: Tragedy reached insurmountable levels on Monday, when twenty-one-year-old Suzanne Sharma jumped into the pyre of her late boyfriend, Hari Singh Sandhu, and committed sati. Hari had died while saving her and many other foreign nationals in the Mumbai terror attacks on 26 November. The couple was dining at Taj Mahal Hotel's premier restaurant Sea Lounge when terrorists opened fire at the innocent guests.

This is the first ever reported case of a girl jumping into her boyfriend's pyre in India's recent history. The girl could not be rescued as flames touched the sky when she suddenly jumped in wearing a red salwaar kameez. Suzanne, a BA second year student of GCG, was the daughter of Professor and Mrs Devender Sharma of Sector-34.

Suzanne's best friend, Gaitri Singh, in an exclusive interview to this correspondent said, 'I had the opportunity to spend a few minutes with my friend before the horrific incident. I think the Mumbai attacks had left a deep scar on her mind because just before she jumped into the pyre, she had told me that Hari was a reincarnation of Maharaja Ranjit Singh.' Ms Singh also claimed to know Hari intimately and said that they had broken off due to a misunderstanding.

Incidentally, Captain W. Osborne, while describing the funeral obsequies of Ranjit Singh, who died in 1839 at the age of fifty-nine, in a letter had written the following:

> His four wives, all very handsome, burnt themselves with his body, as did five of his Kashmiri slave girls, one of whom was called the Lotus, or Lily, and who I

often saw last year in my first visit to Lahore.

One year later...

For Shamsher, his world had come to an end. His stoop, full grey beard, and signs of Parkinson's while sipping tea suggested he was losing the will to live. With both sons having died at very young ages, vast tracts of land, fat bank deposits and a stable of fancy cars had become meaningless to Shamsher. He would spend most of his time either in his study gazing at his sons' pictures, or sunning himself in the back lawn and reading books on history, religion, and philosophy.

'Sardar sahib, koi gori ladki milne aai hai. Bazoo mein bacha tana hai (Sardar Sahib, some young foreign girl has come to meet you. She has a child with her),' said Chander Bhan.

'Kya kehti hai (What is she saying)? Send her in,' said Shamsher, who was sitting in his lawn and reading *Empire of the Sikhs* that Hari had bought last year.

The glittering lights and the high-pitched beats of dhol surprised the neighbours as they wondered what could be the reason for this sudden celebration at the Sandhu household.

'I will name this child Ranjit. God willing, this bright blue-eyed Ranjit will once again take charge of Punjab's destiny that congenitally has become self-destructive. May Punjab rise from the ashes, once again,' said Shamsher, unable to hold back his tears, as he embraced the child and Suzanne, accepting them as his grandson and daughter-in-law respectively.

—◦◉◦—

The teenager that he was, Hari, unable to resist Suzanne, had succumbed to lust after their return from Thetford.

Bibliography

Fakir Syed Waheeduddin, *The Real Ranjit Singh*. Patiala: Publication Bureau, Punjabi University, 2001.

Patwant Singh and Jyoti M. Rai, *Empire of the Sikhs: The Life and Times of Maharaja Ranjit Singh*. New Delhi: Hay House, 2010.

Khushwant Singh, *Ranjit Singh: Maharaja of Punjab*. New Delhi: Penguin, 2008.

W.G. Osborne, *Ranjit Singh: The Lion of the Punjab*. New Delhi: Rupa & Co., 2002.

Griffin, Sir Lepel, *Maharaja Ranjit Singh*. Oxford: Clarendon Press, 1892.